BULLY TROUBLE

OCTAVIA JUNE

Bullies of Ember High Series
Book Two

BULLY TROUBLE

Octavia June

Copyright © 2020 Octavia June

This is a work of fiction. Names, characters, places, and incidents either are products of the author's imagination or are used fictitiously. Any resemblance to actual events or locales or persons, living or dead, is entirely coincidental.

https://octaviajune.weebly.com/

I stopped in the middle of the school hallway when I saw a familiar face with the principal. It was Rhys' father, and he was wearing his cop uniform, which probably meant he was here on official business rather than just to talk about his son.

Everyone in school was still talking about what had been posted on the secret, private website called the Ember High Journal that someone had created for our school so they could share all kinds of things, mostly gossip.

All the students and anyone who had the password could access it and comment on the posts, but only the admin could post news and fully control the website.

I'd found out Rhys was the admin, or had been, since the latest news that had been posted probably wasn't something he'd ever want to go public. Someone else had gained access to it and posted Rhys', Zack's, Ethan's, and Aaron's secrets.

A part of me wondered if it had all been a mistake. Maybe Rhys had been writing about their secrets for whatever reason and accidentally uploaded the file to the website. But that seemed like a wild theory, especially since the boys were blaming me for the whole thing.

And yeah, I'd had access to Rhys' computer while he'd been logged in, but I hadn't changed the password or posted anything. All I'd wanted was to know the identity of the person who was behind it.

Even though the boys tried to pretend that everything that had been posted about them on the website was a lie, I didn't think anyone believed them.

And now the cops were here. I'd been doing my best to avoid the boys after they'd attacked me, but I wanted to know what was going on.

Inching closer to the principal and Rhys' father, I strained my ears while I pretended I was busy with something on my phone.

"It won't be easy to take down that website," the principal said. "Our legal department is working on it, but it looks like the website is hosted in some country overseas, and removing it sounds almost impossible. We can block access to it from the computers in our school, but that's about it. It's possible the owner isn't even a student here. I heard the students are the ones who've been anonymously submitting content and information. We're going to have a chat with them, and some extra classes about bullying and online behavior."

"My colleagues and I are doing our best to find the person responsible," Rhys' father said. "The lies about my family that were posted on that website are malicious. Someone who also wants to damage my family's and my reputation is behind it. I'm going to find them and bring them to justice."

"I don't understand who would ever write such things," the principal said. "We all appreciate everything you're doing for our community. I can't imagine someone would want to hurt your family like that."

"I guess it's someone I caught committing a crime, or maybe someone whose family member I rightfully put in jail."

"Yes, that would make sense. Only a criminal would run such a vile website." The principal kept nodding.

"I'll keep you informed, but rest assured we won't let those responsible get away with this," Rhys' father said with a small smile.

"Thank you. I don't know what we would've done without you."

"Ah, one more thing before I go. My son couldn't come to school today. I'd like to excuse his absence. He was so shocked and angry about the lies posted about our family that he had an accident and hurt himself."

The principal gasped in surprise. "Oh, is he okay?"

"He has two broken ribs and some bruises, but luckily, he'll be fine."

"I'm glad he's going to be fine, and you don't have to worry. He should stay home until he feels better. I'll talk to his teachers to make sure he doesn't fall behind."

"That's so generous of you. Thank you." Rhys' father inclined his head.

"I won't keep you any longer," the principal said. "Hopefully, the next time we speak, this nightmare will be over."

I glared at Rhys' father, my fingers clenching.

What had he done to Rhys? Had he found out that Rhys had had access to the website? Or had he just been angry his secret was out, even if no one believed it, and he'd taken his fury out on his son again?

I didn't think Rhys had just randomly fallen and cracked his ribs. If Aaron and Ethan were being investigated for using forbidden substances because of what had been posted on the website, then why were the claims about Rhys' father ignored and instantly discarded?

So what if Rhys' father was charming and nice to everyone? I couldn't understand it. But even if someone reported it to the cops, his buddies at work would cover for him or protect him, as they probably wouldn't believe it either because they supposedly knew him well.

As Rhys' father turned to go to the exit, he glanced at me. I stopped breathing for a second, expecting him to come to me, but he didn't even spare me a second glance.

Maybe he didn't know everything. Maybe Rhys hadn't told him that the boys suspected me. I supposed Rhys couldn't say anything because then his father would ask him how he knew about it and how I'd gotten all that info.

It would be difficult to explain, even if he came up with some story. Or maybe the last thing Rhys wanted was his father's help. Obviously, his father didn't even want to help him. All he wanted was to make his life more difficult.

For a few moments, I thought about what the boys had told me when they'd confronted me. Rhys had mentioned I was the only one who'd had access to his computer because my prints were there, but I had no idea how he could've gotten my prints, especially without his father's help.

He'd probably lied to me about it so I'd get worried

and think the cops were onto me too. All the boys had wanted was for me to confess.

I could understand they needed someone to blame, but it hurt that they'd turned on me so easily and so quickly, without even waiting to hear what I had to say about the whole thing.

If they kept insisting I was guilty, it still wasn't too late for one of them to tell the cops about me. I didn't know if I wanted to talk to Rhys' father or not.

Sure, I knew I was innocent, and no one would be able to find any evidence to blame me for the whole thing, but I didn't trust Rhys' father at all.

And the boys...

This was going to destroy them. Rhys had already suffered the consequences. If Ethan's football team and Aaron's soccer team managed to confirm that the boys had been using steroids, drugs, or whatever to improve their performance, they were going to get kicked off their teams.

Only a few days ago, they'd been the kings of the school, and almost everyone secretly wanted to be them or be in their company, but now they were a laughing stock.

It was like everyone had finally gotten a chance to find a bunch of faults in the boys' apparently flawless lives, and their godlike status had been destroyed.

The boys had bullied a lot of students, including me, and many probably saw what was happening to them as karma.

A payback for everything they'd done.

But I couldn't help but feel bad for them. It sucked being ridiculed on that website. I knew that first-hand, but I'd also gotten to know a different side of the boys too.

They could do so much better.

They could be so much better.

And yet, I dreaded seeing them again because I didn't want them to take their frustrations out on me again. Maybe they'd see reason and figure out that it couldn't have been me who'd posted their secrets, even if I'd known about them.

Just like I could've found out everything, someone else could've done the same. We should all be focusing on figuring out who it was, because that person had the power now.

If we were lucky, they'd shut the website, but it didn't look like that was going to happen. I just hoped they wouldn't be posting any more stuff about anyone.

We'd had enough bullying around here.

It was time for it to end.

CHAPTER 2

"Hey!" Ethan's furious green eyes were trained on me as he dashed across the hallway, his blond hair disheveled. "You have to take that shit down!"

I wanted to get away from him, but I was too slow. And Zack showed up a second later from behind me, shoving me toward Ethan. Aaron was approaching too, his hazel eyes filled with anger.

I backed away, but I collided with the wall. The three boys surrounded me like sharks.

"It wasn't me. You have to believe me." I gave them a pleading look.

Zack's dark brown eyes were unyielding, and Aaron raked his hand through his brown hair as he looked down the hallway, probably to check if anyone was coming to my rescue.

"Goddammit, Melody." Ethan slammed his fist against the wall very close to my head, making me wince. "Don't you see how serious the situation is? Do you know what happened to Rhys because of you? Do you know!?" he spat.

"We can still reach an agreement," Aaron said. "Just take that damn thing down! You've already ruined our lives enough!"

"I didn't do anything!" I raised my voice. "I swear!"

"Do you think this is a game, huh?" Zack got into my face. "Do you think we're just going to let you do this to us? That you're going to walk away laughing and pretending you don't have a clue what we're talking about?" His hand shot out and wrapped around my neck.

My eyes widened, my heart thumping loudly in my chest. I caught his wrist, but he was too strong, and I couldn't pull his fingers away from my throat.

"Remove everything you wrote or you're done," Zack breathed, his face serious.

"Let go of me!" Panic filled my whole body, and I thrashed against him.

"Hey, get the fuck away from her!" Samantha's voice

cut through the air. "Get the fuck away, or I'm going to call the whole school and the cops—"

As Sam kept shouting at them, Zack dropped his hand, and I gasped for breath.

The boys glared at Sam and the dark-haired, dark-eyed boy who shyly stood behind her as if he couldn't understand what was going on but was sure he didn't want any part of it anyway.

"This isn't over." Aaron pointed his finger at me. "You don't know what's coming for you if you don't do as we say."

The three of them stormed off, and Sam ran to me, her brown eyes filled with worry, her curly brown hair flying around her.

"Oh, my god, Mel. Are you okay?" She placed her hand on my shoulder, looking me up and down.

"I am now. Thanks. If you haven't shown up—" I really didn't know what I would've done or how I could've reasoned with the boys when they didn't want to hear any of what I had to say.

Getting them to believe me without proof seemed impossible. But how could I prove I hadn't done anything?

"What the fuck is wrong with them? What did they want? I thought they weren't—" Sam said.

"I thought we were friends too, but for some reason,

they think I'm the one who posted that stuff about them."

"What?" Her eyebrows shot up. "Why the hell would they think that?"

"I don't know. I guess because I was the only one around them." I bit down on my lip, wondering if I should tell her about Rhys. "One of them had access to the website, and it logged me in when I was using his computer."

Sam's eyes widened. "One of them? Of course it was one of them! Ugh! They're such assholes. So who else has access?"

I shrugged. "I don't know if they were all running the website together or what, but I think someone got their password and changed it, so they can't log back in. The same person posted all that stuff. I don't know how they got the info, but—"

"Maybe other students submitted that info over time, but obviously those four idiots didn't want their secrets out, so they didn't post anything. If someone else has access to all the comments and submissions, they could've found out something. But those bullies have been posting shit about people for years. Don't they think pretty much everyone they posted about might want revenge? Why only blame you?"

"I don't know." I wasn't comfortable talking about kissing the boys and getting closer with them just yet.

I doubted any of it had anything to do with what had happened, but maybe it was why they were more likely to be hurt by my supposed betrayal.

And maybe I was deluding myself, and they'd been trying to trick me and now believed I'd found out and retaliated before they could've fully executed their plan.

But they hadn't said anything about that, so it could just be my wild imagination.

"You know what you need? Protection," Sam said. "I'm not going to let you out of my sight, and I'm not going to let any of those bullies anywhere near you."

"That sounds good, actually." I didn't want to find myself in trouble again, especially because the boys refused to believe me or even hear me out.

"Oh, I almost forgot." She glanced over her shoulder at the boy, who was still awkwardly standing behind her. "This is Keith. He's new here."

"Hi." Keith gave me a little wave.

I offered him a small smile. "Hi. Nice to meet you."

"They usually don't accept transfer students at this point, but he's an exception. His parents are in the military," Sam said and stepped closer to Keith. "Hey, how about we form a club that fights bullies? Something like an anti-bully club? Keith, I know this is all probably super-scary to you, but I assure you, we're not totally crazy and our school isn't a zoo. It's just that we have these four popular, super-hot boys who think they're gods. Except, everyone just recently found out their lives aren't so awesome and perfect like they pretend."

Keith's jaw went slack as he stared at her. "Um, okay."

"I have a lot to tell you. First, about the Ember High Journal, and then— Wait, I just got an idea." She spun toward me, glancing at Keith. "Sorry, Keith, but I just have to do this first."

"It's fine. You can tell me everything later." He waved his hand in dismissal.

"Awesome." She flashed him a smile and focused back on me. "What was I saying? Ah, yeah. Do you think we could figure out who has control of the Ember High Journal now? I mean, Zack, Aaron, Ethan, and Rhys obviously don't, and they have no clue who did it. I want to know who has it now, and I'm sure you want the same thing because then you could prove to those imbeciles that they're the stupidest people on this planet for blaming you."

"Yeah, that's a great idea, but how are we going to do that?"

The boys knew a lot of people and their secrets.

Maybe they'd even made deals with some so they wouldn't post anything.

Sure, now their control over everyone was quickly disappearing, but maybe they still had ways to find things out.

Or maybe not, since they were after me. They might be even more furious because of the fact that they couldn't manipulate everyone and do whatever the hell they wanted.

"I don't know yet, but we can come up with something." Sam tilted her head. "We could make a list of the potential suspects. People who were hurt a lot by that website. Those who lost their relationships or had their reputation ruined..."

"Right. We can just find the biggest incident and start from there." I didn't look forward to searching through all the horrible things that had been posted on the website, but it wasn't like we had many options.

"Yeah. Wasn't there a girl who actually switched to another school because there was a link to her sex tape or something?"

"I think so." That definitely sounded like something worth investigating.

If it had happened to me, I would've wanted revenge no matter what it took.

"Okay, then we're going to start with that. Keith, wanna help?" Sam said.

"Um, I don't know. I don't really know anyone here."

"Well, this is one of the ways to meet them," Sam said and cringed. "Not a really good way, but—"

"I can try," Keith said.

"Okay. Let's do this," Sam said.

CHAPTER 3

I left Sam and Keith after school so I could try to visit Rhys. Maybe he'd be more willing to hear me out, and I wanted to make sure he was okay.

I couldn't exactly ask any of the boys how he was, and I doubted he'd respond if I texted him.

Hell, I didn't even know if he still had his phone with him or if his father had taken it away. Going to his house to check was a bit scary, and I didn't know if his father was going to be there too, but I had to do it.

Even if Rhys refused to listen to me, I'd at least find out if he was all right. Unless his father stopped me from seeing him.

Sam and Keith were still trying to figure out who might be controlling the Ember High Journal now, but it seemed like an impossible task. We'd gone through a lot of content, and we'd come up with a huge list of people.

Any of them could be behind it all. And hell, what Rhys and the rest of the boys had done with that website was terrible, so I couldn't blame any of their victims for wanting to get justice in this way, but now the website should be shut down before more people got hurt.

As I waited for someone to open the front door, I glanced around. There were now curtains hiding all the windows, as far as I could see.

I supposed Rhys' father didn't want to risk anything anymore. Maybe he'd used Rhys' well-being as an excuse, even though I was sure he didn't give a damn about that. He only cared about himself and how the whole thing made him look.

When the door opened, Rhys' father flashed me a welcoming smile. Knowing what he was really like made that smile seem even more chilling.

"Hi, Mr. Blake," I said, faking a smile too. "I don't know if you remember me, but I'm Rhys' friend from school, Melody. Our teacher instructed me to bring homework to him and show him what we did in class today. Can I come in?"

The teacher hadn't told me anything, but it wasn't like Rhys' father would know I was lying, and I had actually made copies of our homework and some school stuff for Rhys.

"Yes, of course. But give me a moment to let him know you're here," he said.

I nodded and stepped inside.

There was a huge chance Rhys' father would tell me that Rhys was sleeping or something so I couldn't see him, but he couldn't come up with lies forever and expect me to believe them, could he?

I chewed on the inside of my cheek. There was also a chance Rhys would tell his father he didn't want to see me.

"Come on." Rhys' father waved at me. "But don't take too long. My son needs rest."

"Yeah, sure." I flashed him a quick smile.

When I poked my head in Rhys' room, I spotted Rhys in bed, his head turned away from me and toward the window, or well, the thick curtain that was in the way.

"Hey," I said softly as I entered and closed the door behind me.

Rhys' father was probably going to be very close in the hallway and try to listen in on us, so I had to keep my voice down.

"What the fuck do you want?" When Rhys' blue eyes turned to me, they were full of hurt and annoyance. "Came here to gloat?"

"No. Why would I do that? I know you think I had something to do with what was posted online, but it wasn't me. I swear." I opened my bag and pulled out a few sheets of paper. "I brought you homework."

"Just leave me alone."

"Why do you think it was me? There has to be some proof that I didn't change anything or had any way to find out what your password was."

"Leave me the fuck alone!" he shouted.

"Okay, fine." I didn't want his father to come check what was going on. "But at least take this." I offered him the papers.

He made a move as if he was going to take them, but something clinked, and he let out a frustrated groan and lay back on the pillows.

"Sorry, are you in pain? I can just put them on your —" I went quiet.

The covers had moved out of place, and I saw a cuff on Rhys' left wrist. It was attached to the bed. ,

His gaze followed mine.

"Get out!" he snapped.

"Do you need help? Maybe I can—"

"Get the fuck out!"

I quickly tossed the papers onto his desk and dashed for the door. He didn't want me here, so I definitely shouldn't stay and try to force him to talk to me.

But seeing him like this broke my heart. Rhys was probably in pain, because I didn't think the story about his cracked ribs was fake, and his father had cuffed him to the bed too.

What kind of monster did that to their own child?

I gritted my teeth when I got out into the hallway. Rhys' father was waiting for me at the end. Shit.

If only I could confront him and tell him he was the worst piece of shit I'd ever met. But if I said something even remotely close to that, I could end up getting arrested, and Rhys would be in even more trouble.

No one would believe me if I told them what I'd seen. Maybe even Rhys would be pressured into denying everything.

"Thank you for doing this," Rhys' father said. "I'm sure my son appreciates it."

"No problem. I'm glad I can help." It took all my willpower to pretend nothing was going on.

"Before you go, I'd like to have a chat with you."

Oh shit.

"Sure." I couldn't exactly say no, could I?

"Do you know anything about the Ember High Journal?"

"Um, yeah. It's some stupid website everyone at school is talking about. People post gossip and stuff like that on there."

"Do you know who might be running it?" His eyes were trained on me, and I had a feeling he was watching me carefully for even the slightest reaction.

Maybe he was a shit human being, but he was probably a not-so-terrible cop.

"No." At least that was the truth.

"Have you noticed anyone behaving unusually at your school? Maybe becoming more secretive? Or more involved in gossip?"

"No, I don't think so. But we have a lot of exams and stuff to worry about, so most of us don't have time for that stuff."

"You're a good kid, Melody. I can tell. But not everyone is like you, so you should be careful."

"Yes, of course, Mr. Blake."

"All right then." He clapped me on the shoulder. "If you hear anything or find out anything, you can always call me and let me know. Your safety and the safety of all the other students is what matters most, and the person behind that website is hurting a lot of people. They need to be stopped."

I nodded.

It was funny that he cared about the safety of students, but that somehow didn't include his son.

Or maybe he thought that he was the only one who had the exclusive right to hurt Rhys, and no one else. I wouldn't be surprised if that was his twisted logic.

I got out of that house as fast as I could, mumbling a quick goodbye to Rhys' father. It made me furious that Rhys still thought I was the one who'd exposed his secrets, and that there was nothing I could do to help him.

First, I had to prove my innocence, which was crazy considering there wasn't even any real proof against me, but it was the only way I could get close to the boys again.

And then we could try to figure out something to save Rhys together. I was probably an idiot for even being willing to give them a chance after they'd all ganged up on me so easily, but I couldn't help myself.

I wanted them to know the truth, and then I'd figure out if it was worth it to try to at least stay friends with them.

CHAPTER 4

"You know what?" Sam said from the other end of the line, and I clutched my phone tighter in my hand. "I'm starting to think again that one of them is behind this mess, even if they did expose their own secrets. I mean, they accused you of being in Rhys' house, but I bet they were all there too. So why aren't they suspecting one of them?"

She took a deep breath. "Hell, maybe they all had the password to begin with. Who says one of them didn't get mad about something and changed it? It would be hard for someone to get inside Rhys' house and get the password. How do they even think you did it? Did he have it written on his mirror or something?"

"I don't know," I said.

"And why are they blaming you as if no one else could've done what you supposedly have done? The whole thing seems fishy to me, especially when they have, like, the whole school full of potential suspects. Do they really think no one would've dared to break in and change the password? You said Rhys was logged in when you opened the website on his computer. That's like Stupidity 101."

"Maybe, but how can we know any of that? The guilty one won't just come out and tell us."

"That's the difficult part. Let me think about it. I'll call you later."

"Okay. Bye." I ended the call.

Even if Sam believed one of the boys could be responsible, my gut instinct told me it was unlikely.

Yeah, maybe they were weirded out about me kissing all of them, but those boys had always been very close, like family. I didn't think they would hurt one another like that.

It just wasn't who they were.

But maybe I was wrong.

Maybe I wanted to believe there was good in them because of what I might or might not feel for them. I didn't want to think about that at all right now.

Not until I figured out the truth.

As for the boys, maybe I could do something. I'd finished my homework, and there was still time. I could pay the rest of the boys a visit. Without them knowing.

Stalking them and spying on them sounded terrible, but they wouldn't talk to me or admit the truth. If it was all some game they were all playing for some reason and they were using me, then I needed to know about it.

And I wasn't going to follow them around all the time or anything. Ugh, how much mental gymnastics was it going to take for me to stop feeling like a creep?

Because what I was planning to do was all kinds of creepy.

After I got dressed, I hurried out.

Ethan's house was the first place I intended to check. Maybe the boys were outside or visiting Rhys, but I supposed I was going to find out.

I had no idea if Aaron, Zack, and Ethan were allowed to see Rhys, or if his father had decided to keep them away.

When I reached the house, I hid behind the trees and bushes, and slowly inched closer.

A few moments later, I spotted Ethan and Zack sitting on a small bench in the backyard. I did my best to stay as still and as quiet as possible, and hoped they wouldn't spot me.

If they did, they'd probably be even more convinced that I'd spilled their secrets to the whole school.

A car passing close by made it impossible for me to hear any of what they were saying, but once it was gone, I strained my ears.

"I wish Aaron and Rhys were here," Ethan said. "We should be doing something, not just wasting our time sitting on our asses."

"I agree, but you know how Rhys' dad is. He's not going to let us go anywhere near him, at least not until he cools down. And Aaron told me his mom and dad totally flipped when they heard he got kicked off the team. They're not going to let him out either. If we want to do something, we'll have to do it without them."

"Fuck." Zack ran his hand over his face, then groaned as his phone rang. "My mom again. I don't know what the hell she wants. Did she forget she kicked me out of her precious, empty house? I'm not going back there, and I'm not playing her pretense game ever again. She actually wrote a whole post on Facebook about the *lies*, and she claims our house will be put on sale after renovations. It's ridiculous."

"You can stay here for as long as you want," Ethan said.

"Thanks, man."

I ducked behind a bush, wondering about what I'd

just heard. So Aaron was sort of on house arrest too. Even if he wanted to quit soccer, I didn't think he'd expose his secret to do it, especially when he knew his parents would lose their minds.

Besides, he actually liked playing too. Maybe not as competitively as his parents wanted, but I didn't think he'd hurt his friends just to get out of it.

Ethan could've just quit the football team on his own, or stop worrying about disappointing his parents and about his brother always being the golden child. I didn't think he had any real motives to want to ruin his friends either.

But Zack... He'd wanted to expose his family's secret and get away from them. Although, he could've just posted the truth online himself, without involving anyone else. It would've had the same effect.

No, I didn't think it was him either. The whole thing that had happened had probably only given him the courage he needed to get away.

"What about *her*?" Zack suddenly asked, and my shoulders stiffened. "What are we going to do about Mel? Do you think she's telling the truth?"

Ethan lowered his voice, so I couldn't hear a thing. Shit!

Zack and Ethan whispered something, and then they

got up and disappeared through the front door. I wasn't going to find out anything anymore. Ugh.

Keeping my head down, I rushed away from there before someone saw me. It was risky to stick around anyway.

But a part of me wondered just how comfortable and careless the boys had gotten. Even now, after everything, they'd been talking out in the open where everyone could've overheard them.

Hell, I'd found out stuff about them by accident just because I'd happened to be around. Someone else could've done the same. If someone had been watching them, they could've not only found out their secrets but also gotten control of the website.

It was really foolish of the boys to only consider me as a suspect, even if Rhys had been the only one who'd been logged in while the others hadn't.

How were they so sure no one had hacked them? Just because they'd been running that damn website didn't mean they were tech experts.

But maybe they weren't only considering me. Maybe there were others, but they were only going after me because they wanted the real culprit to believe they weren't onto them until they had proof or a plan on how to deal with them.

But why not tell me anything then? I'd have made my act realistic rather than be freaked out by them.

I didn't want to be afraid of them or worry about what they were going to do next. And yeah, I kept hoping they believed me and trusted me, despite constantly being shown that wasn't the case.

I really was an idiot.

CHAPTER 5

I came to school early the next morning so I could meet up with Sam and Keith to see if they'd come up with a plan or figured something out.

But even though I'd gone through our list of potential suspects myself, I didn't even know where to begin.

I didn't really know many of those people to be able to tell if they were behaving any differently or not, and too many were gloating about the boys' downfall anyway. It could be pretty much anyone.

"Hey, you're Melody, right?" A blonde who was in my Biology class this year approached me.

We hadn't really talked much.

Hell, I was surprised she even knew who I was, because I couldn't remember her name.

"Um, yeah." I eyed her carefully.

"Tanner wants to see you in the lab."

"Oh, okay." I had no idea what my teacher wanted, but I could go check now, before I went looking for Sam.

The lab door was closed, so I knocked before opening the door. When I poked my head inside, something cold and wet fell all over me.

I gasped and squinted so the pink liquid wouldn't end up in my eyes. It was everywhere, and it smelled like paint.

My hair was full of it, my clothes, my face...

Barely able to see anything in front of me, I tried to get to the bathroom. I vaguely knew how to get there, but I heard giggling and laughing.

No one tried to help me or asked me if I was okay. If I wasn't wrong, someone had their phone out and was filming the whole thing.

I stumbled to the bathroom, touching the wall and probably leaving paint all over it. Somehow, I made it to the sink, and after I washed the paint out of my face, I looked at my reflection in the mirror.

Fuck. My hair was completely sticky and heavy with paint. Not even one blond strand was visible. It was all pink.

I'd been tricked.

My Biology teacher didn't need me. It had all been a setup and I'd fallen for it. Now there was no way I could go to class, so I pulled out my phone to call my mom. Hopefully, she or Dad could come pick me up.

Once I got out of the hallway, everyone was laughing at me and whispering. Someone even made pig noises.

Ugh. I hated this school so much sometimes.

I could already picture seeing this whole thing online. The Ember High Journal was going to be all over this, even if the interest faded after a few hours.

But who had done this to me? Did I even have to guess?

The boys.

It had to have been them.

No one else would just target me, especially if they somehow believed that I was the one controlling the Journal.

But what were the boys trying to achieve? Weren't they afraid I'd just post more stuff about them? Or, were all of their most important secrets out there, so they didn't care anymore?

I strode down the hallway, doing my best to ignore everyone, even though the corners of my eyes stung with tears.

MY WHOLE FACE WAS ITCHY, AND THERE WERE RED wheals on my forehead and cheeks.

It'd turned out I was allergic to the paint, so now I had to stay home for a day or two until the pills I'd gotten from my doctor cleared up my allergy.

My mom knocked on the open door of my room before entering.

"Honey, how are you feeling?" she asked.

"I'm fine, I guess. It's just itchy." It had taken me a few hours to get all the paint out of my hair too, and I had no idea if it would ever get out of my clothes.

"Don't scratch it. You don't want to make it worse or infected."

"I'm trying." I'd actually scratched at my bed covers, even if doing that didn't relieve the itching, but I'd had to do something with my hands or I'd have gone crazy.

"The medicine will kick in soon. You'll feel better. You'll see." She sat down on the edge of my bed. "But there's something I need to talk to you about. What exactly happened at school? The principal said it was a prank."

Of course the principal thought it was just a stupid prank, even if it had ended up having more consequences than anyone expected.

Hell, I hadn't been aware either that I was allergic to

a certain type of paint because I'd never come in contact with it like this before.

"I don't know. I guess, yeah, it was a prank." If I said anything more than that, my mom would want me to give her all the information, and I didn't want to do that just yet.

I didn't want her to go after the boys or call the principal about it. I had no proof the boys had done anything, and it looked like they hadn't even been in school so early.

Maybe they still had some control over someone, and they'd used it. Or maybe they'd found someone who pitied them and had convinced them I was the worst person that had ever existed.

"Who would do something like that?" my mom asked. "I understand minor pranks, but this is serious. What if you'd had a more serious reaction? What if you'd gotten injured? It wasn't a harmless prank and I told your principal that. But all everyone says is that the girl who told you to go to the lab can't help because she doesn't remember who informed her that the teacher needed you. She said that someone approached her and told her to give you a message, and she did."

Right.

Claiming not to know or not being able to recognize

the person who said it sounded like such a nice cop-out, although maybe she really hadn't been paying attention.

Perhaps the boys were still in control of everything. Just because they didn't have access to the website anymore didn't mean they didn't have a backup of certain info, and they could still be using it for blackmail.

"I don't know. I guess someone wasn't thinking." I shrugged.

"But why you? Is anyone bothering you? Is there something going on that you haven't told me about? You know you can tell me anything. If someone is bullying you, I need to know. It might not seem like I can do anything to help, but I assure you that I can."

"I know, Mom. But these pranks happen. Maybe it was because I was one of the rare people who got to school early, so I was the first to run into that girl. We have a class together, so she somewhat knows me." I hated lying to my mom, but even I wasn't sure just yet the boys were the ones responsible.

I was obviously delusional, but whatever.

"Okay." My mom sighed. "Let's hope this won't happen again."

"Yeah."

"I'll leave you to rest. If you need anything, just shout for me." She gave me a small smile.

"Thanks, Mom." I smiled back.

When she was gone, I grabbed my laptop. Once I opened my inbox, an email caught my eye.

It had been sent from an email address I didn't recognize, and the subject was my name. What the hell?

I clicked it open, half wondering if it was a virus that was going to infect my whole computer. When I read through it, my jaw went slack.

It was a threat.

If you don't fix what you messed up, things will only get worse for you. Today was just the beginning. You'll pay for everything you've done.

The email wasn't signed and there was no way to figure out who the sender was. It was probably a throwaway account so that I couldn't report them, but it had to be the boys.

Unless someone was pretending to be them to create an even greater rift between us, but I didn't think that was the case.

It was them.

They were the ones who'd orchestrated everything so the paint would spill all over me, and now they were threatening me.

Except, I couldn't do anything about that damn website.

Speaking of the website, I closed my inbox and open

the Ember High Journal. I braced myself because I was sure someone had submitted a video of me getting paint all over me.

But as I clicked through the latest posts, I couldn't find anything. Huh. Maybe it was still too early. But there was some recent news too.

It was possible I wasn't interesting enough, although that probably wasn't it. And it looked like the person who controlled the website now still kept posting regular stuff, so they clearly weren't just after revenge.

Maybe they liked being in control and messing with other people like they'd been messed with. But why not post the video of me then?

Now the boys were going to be sure that I was behind it all and that I would never post something that would be used to make fun of me.

I closed my laptop and leaned back on my pillows.

Ah, shit.

I was in even deeper trouble than I'd thought.

CHAPTER 6

I intently stared at my phone, my fingers hovering over the screen.

How could I get the boys to stop tormenting me for something I hadn't done? Since they refused to listen to me when I tried to talk to them in person, maybe a text would work.

I still had their numbers, but I had no idea if they'd blocked me. I supposed there was only one way to find out, but first, I had to come up with something smart to say.

Something that wouldn't make me look guilty in the boys' eyes.

I started a few sentences but deleted them all. Biting down on my lip, I tried again. It turned into an essay, so I figured I might as well email it instead.

Hey, guys. I know you hate me at the moment, but please let me explain. You owe me that much. I don't control the Ember High Journal. If I did, I would've taken it down immediately.

I don't know why you think I had something to do with that. If you don't have access to the site anymore, it can be for many reasons. Someone could've hacked you or found a way to steal the password or whatever you were using to control the website.

I don't even know how I could've done something. I know Rhys says that I opened the website on his computer, and yeah, I did that. But I didn't change anything. I don't know when and how I could've done it.

I don't think the password was openly written anywhere for me to snatch, and if it was, then obviously anyone could've taken it. It hurts that you blame me for this. You have a ton of enemies, and I'm not one of them.

Well, at least I'd like not to be one of them. I thought we had something. A special moment between you guys and me at the party.

I don't know why you think I would want to destroy your lives or that I'd risk getting expelled during my senior year if someone caught me editing that damn website. It's crazy.

If you don't believe me, fine. But don't attack me without proof. Actually, I'd like to help you figure out who did it.

I'm willing to forgive you for causing my allergy and

embarrassing me with that paint (I know it was you, so don't bother denying it) if you apologize and stop accusing me of something I didn't and couldn't have done.

Melody

I read through the email a billion times, wondering if it was too long and too stupid. Probably both, but I didn't know how else to say everything I wanted to say, and if I started talking about all the other things, I'd write a whole book.

This email would have to do. If the boys still refused to see reason, then I'd have to think about protecting myself from them.

I'd have to stop feeling sorry for them or try to understand them. I'd have to think about myself first, because if I didn't, things could get ugly.

Only a few minutes after I pressed the send button, an email appeared in my inbox. It was from Rhys.

Why did you run from the party? It all happened right after you left. You played us once, but it won't happen again.

I furrowed my brow.

I called my mom and went straight home. You can ask her if you want, and I'm pretty sure my neighbors saw me too.

I don't know how I could've gotten to Rhys' house and done I don't even know what. And the reason I ran from the party...

My fingers hesitated over the screen.

It was because I was overwhelmed. The kisses we shared made me feel all kinds of different things and I was confused. I needed time to think and clear my head. I'm not used to feeling that way.

I'm sorry I just left like that, but it was the only thing I could've done at that moment. I don't want to lose the connection we share. I don't think you want that either.

I bit down on my lip while waiting for another answer.

Another email. This time from Zack.

Are you serious right now? It was all just a game. There's nothing between us. Are you really that dumb to believe any of us would like someone like you?

Tears prickled the corners of my eyes, and I was moments away from throwing my phone across the room.

But it wasn't my phone's fault my boys were idiots.

My boys.

It looked like they weren't mine anymore. Actually, they were my enemies now.

I reread the email. Okay, this was all I needed to finally stop hoping things would work themselves out.

I was done trying to convince the boys that I hadn't done anything wrong, and I definitely wasn't going to apologize or try to explain anything. If anyone should do any of that, it was them.

If you think I'm the only one who would want to hurt you, you're all dumber than I thought.

I angrily typed the reply and sent it, and then I closed the email app.

Done.

They could all go to hell for all I cared.

I did still want to find out who had taken over the website. Not because of the boys, but because of everyone else.

It didn't look like the person in question was going to stop posting things, and just because they hadn't posted a video of me didn't mean a thing.

Maybe simply no one had submitted it. And even if I somehow had protection for whatever reason, which I doubted, that website still had to be taken down.

No more lives should be ruined because of it. If people wanted to gossip, they could do it in the hallways like they'd always done.

But even though I wanted to stop thinking about the boys, I couldn't. There was a hole in my chest, and a worm of doubt entered my brain.

What if Zack had told me the truth?

They could've been playing me, and I could've

imagined the whole thing. Boys like them weren't into girls like me. Maybe just for fun or tricks, but not for anything else.

I'd been an idiot for thinking they liked me. I'd been an idiot to think that I was somehow special.

A knock on the door almost made me jump.

"Come in." My voice was slightly hoarse.

My mom entered the room. "Hey, honey. Are you okay? Your eyes look a little—"

"I'm fine. I guess it's just my allergy leftover." The pills were working, and I should be able to go back to school tomorrow.

Dread filled my stomach at the thought of seeing any of the boys.

"If you're still not feeling perfectly fine, I'll call the school and—"

"No, Mom. It's okay."

"All right. I actually came here to tell you that the school wants you to speak to the counselor before class tomorrow."

"Oh, okay." I didn't want to talk about what had happened.

Hopefully, the counselor wouldn't insist too much. Maybe we'd just talk about bullying in general and about what I should do in such situations.

"Get some sleep, honey," my mom said. "You don't want to be late tomorrow."

"Yeah." I sighed.

It was going to be a long day.

I could already feel it.

CHAPTER 7

"Is that all?" the counselor asked, his dark eyes narrowed and trained on me. "Are you sure you're not leaving anything out?"

"Um, yeah." I'd told him as much as I could about the incident.

Unless I wanted to accuse the boys without proof, there wasn't anything else left to say. Maybe if they did something to me again, and I had proof or witnesses who were willing to speak out, then I could mention the boys were probably to blame for spilling paint all over me too.

But I didn't want to talk to the counselor about my relationship with the boys or about anything else. I didn't trust him.

"Okay." The counselor jotted down something in his

notebook. "But you have to be at least able to guess who might be behind the prank. Even if you got pranked by accident and it was meant for someone else."

"It wasn't. The *message* was for me. No one saw anything or told me anything, so I don't think I can just make a guess. Are you going to talk to the other students who were at school that morning? Maybe someone saw something." I had no idea why he'd even think it had been intended for someone other than me when that girl had specifically said my name.

Did he believe no one would be interested in pranking me? Was I not popular enough or something?

What the hell?

"I'll talk to a few students who were close by, yes. But before you go, I have another question for you."

I gripped my bag in my hand, annoyed that I couldn't leave.

"Am I wasting my time here?" he asked.

My eyebrows shot up. "Excuse me?"

"Am I wasting my time looking for the person who pranked you?"

"I already told you I—"

"No, I'm not talking about that. Are you the one who arranged the whole thing?"

I gaped at him.

Was he out of his mind?

"No. Why would I even want to do that to myself?"

"I don't know." He shrugged. "Girls like you crave attention."

Girls like me?

What the fuck?

"I didn't prank myself. That's ridiculous. And what do you mean *girls like me*?" If he could explain the fucked up thing that had come out of his mouth, I'd like to see it.

That was beyond unprofessional. I had no clue who'd hired this guy.

He probably knew someone who knew someone, and that was how he'd gotten the job. I didn't have any other explanation.

"Teens, especially girls, love to be in the center of attention. Some are willing to do just about anything to get it. But I'm sure you already know that."

I just stared at him. "Am I free to go?"

"Yes."

"Awesome," I mumbled under my breath, got to my feet, and stormed out of his office.

I couldn't believe he'd accused me of pranking myself to get attention, because I supposed that, as a teenage girl, I just had to be desperate.

Because why would anyone pay any attention to me otherwise?

Any kind of attention, even bad, was good. Yeah right.

That guy was an idiot. If I'd told him the boys were behind it all, he would've probably laughed in my face and said that boys like them would never go to such trouble for a girl like me.

I was so angry I could barely think, so I strode to the bathroom to splash some water on my face.

Just as I was drying my face with a paper towel, I heard the door open and close. When I looked up to see who it was, I almost screamed.

The boys.

All four of them.

They strode toward me with angry looks on their faces.

"Your phone," Ethan said. "Give it to me."

"No. You're not allowed to be in here!" I shouted, hoping someone would hear me. "This is the girls' bathroom."

"We can be anywhere we want," Aaron said. "Now be a good girl and give us your phone."

"No." As soon as the word left my mouth, they rushed me.

I tried to fight them off, but Rhys ripped my bag off my shoulder while the rest were holding me trapped against the sink.

Rhys rummaged through my bag and snatched my phone.

"Unlock it," he said a few moments later.

"I won't!" I had no clue what they wanted from me, but I didn't want to let them use my phone.

Who knew what they were going to do with it if I complied?

"Do it!" Zack's grip on me was so tight that I cried out.

Fighting them was futile, and when Rhys slipped the phone into my hand, I unlocked it.

"Let go of me!" I yelled, but it didn't look like anyone was coming to help me.

It was still too early for Sam to arrive. If I hadn't had a session with the counselor, I would've waited for her. Now I was on my own.

My throat tightened as Rhys grabbed the phone again and was furiously tapping the screen.

"You can't do this to me!" I said. "Let me go!"

"Anything?" Ethan asked, looking at Rhys.

"Nothing," Rhys said through his teeth. "She doesn't have it."

What was it that I didn't have?

The password for the website?

Wow, that was just insane.

The door swung open.

"Hey, what the fuck?" Sam shouted. "Let her go right now or I'll yell for the principal!"

"Shit," Aaron muttered.

They released me, and Rhys tossed my phone at me. I barely managed to catch it.

"What the fuck is the matter with you?" Sam glared at them. "Are you fucking crazy? I should be calling the cops! You can't just assault my friend and get away with it!"

The boys barely spared her an annoyed glance before pushing past her and getting out of the bathroom.

When they were gone, I realized I was shaking.

"Mel, are you okay?" Sam pulled me into her arms. "What did they do? What did they want? We can still talk to the principal or call the cops. I don't give a shit Rhys' dad is one of them. There are other cops too. We'll ask for them."

"I'm fine. And we're not going to call anyone. Not yet."

"Look at yourself." Sadness filled her eyes. "You're trembling! That's not okay! You can't let them get away with this. Tell your mom and dad. Tell any adult. But don't stay quiet."

"I need some time. Time to think and..."

"What's there to think about? Yeah, their situation sucks, but you shouldn't feel sorry for bullies. Just because your life is terrible doesn't mean you have to be a jerk. It's not an excuse."

"Yeah, I know. But if too many people get involved too soon, I don't think we'll find out who controls that website. They might go quiet for a while, and then it will be back up. We need to take it down."

"At what cost? We'll be out of this school soon anyway. It's not our job to catch that person. The school and the cops should do it. I mean, we tried. We tried, and all we got is a huge list of people who might want revenge against their bullies. Maybe we should form a group and fight those four assholes together, but then they'd accuse *us* of bullying, so I don't know. Maybe we should just protect ourselves. Fuck the website and whoever is running it."

"I don't know either." I let out a sigh, starting to feel more like myself again.

"You should've called me and told me you'd be here early." Sam pushed a strand of my hair out of my face. "You can't be alone in this damn place."

"Yeah, you're right. I should have. I just thought—"

"That those idiots would develop a brain overnight? Yeah, right. That's not going to happen, so quit hoping."

Sam was right.

Hoping the boys would see reason was pointless. I'd

seen that over and over again, and I'd make sure they wouldn't catch me alone.

But I still believed we should find out who was the website's admin now, because if we didn't, everyone at school and even future generations would suffer.

Even if that person graduated and left school, that didn't mean they wouldn't pass the website on to someone else or just keep up with the gossip through submissions.

I couldn't let that happen.

Not if I could do something about it.

CHAPTER 8

When I got home, my heart rate sped up. The front door was wide open, and my mom stood on the porch with her hand over her mouth.

"Mom?" I ran to her, wondering what was going on.

Something had to be. She wouldn't be standing out there like that, with worry written all over her face.

"Oh, honey." She quickly wound her arms around me.

"What's going on?" I glanced at the open door, but I couldn't see anything out of the ordinary.

"Someone broke into our house," she said. "The cops are on the way."

"What? Are they still—" My eyes widened.

"No. It's safe. No one's in the house. I already

checked. Your dad is on the way too. Don't worry. Everything's going to be all right."

"Are you sure?"

She nodded. "I wouldn't have even noticed anything if I hadn't opened your door."

"Wait, what do you mean? Someone was in my room?" My shock quickly melted into concern.

"Yeah. I don't know if anything was stolen, but—"

I rushed inside.

If the burglar was no longer in there, then I had to see what had happened to my room. Actually, I already had an idea about who could've broken in.

No one would've gone just for my room, especially if they were looking for valuables. But there were four boys who thought I had the password they needed, and they were desperate enough to do just about anything to get it.

Fuck!

"Honey, wait!" my mom called after me, but I was already racing for my room.

When I reached the door, I gasped.

My room had been turned upside down. My closet was open, and all my things were everywhere on the floor. My drawers were open too, and my stuff was everywhere.

The lamp was broken. My laptop was left turned on

in the middle of the bed. My notebooks and books were spilled everywhere, and ripped pieces of paper were scattered around.

It was obvious this hadn't been done by a random thief.

It was them.

I was a hundred percent sure of it.

"Mrs. Reid?" I heard a familiar voice.

Rhys' father.

Of course.

Call the cops, and you always got him. How wonderful.

He'd probably asked to answer any calls that were somehow related to his son. Did he know what Rhys and his friends had done?

Probably not. I didn't even know if all four boys had been in here, or if one of them had done it.

Maybe Rhys had been keeping watch or something, considering he still had to be in quite a bit of pain, or he hadn't even been here.

My mom went on to explain everything and then brought Rhys' father to my room.

"Hello, Melody," Rhys' father said.

"I don't know who could've done something like this," my mom said. "Do you see this mess? It's like they did it on purpose."

"Have you seen anyone?" he asked.

"No. I don't know how they even got in," my mom said. "Everything else in the house is untouched. It's just my daughter's room."

"Melody, can you tell if anything's missing?"

"I don't think so," I said.

The boys had been looking for the password, not some object they could steal.

"Even her laptop is still here," my mom said. "If it was a thief, then why didn't they take it?"

"It's possible you got here just in time and they had to get away as quickly as possible so they wouldn't get caught," Rhys' father said. "There have been various reports of burglaries in this area in the past six months. If nothing's missing, it's because you got lucky. Were any of your windows open?"

"Um, yeah. In the living room," my mom said. "It was just cracked open. I must've forgotten to close it. And all the locks seemed fine."

"Then they must've gotten in and out through the window."

My mom nodded. "Do you think this might have something to do with the prank my daughter suffered at school?"

"Why do you think that?" Rhys' father frowned.

"I don't know. Nothing was taken. The burglar went

straight to my daughter's room. We don't keep any valuables in here. Why not go to the master bedroom? Or our safe? I checked, and everything's untouched. If they entered through the window, the bedroom would be closer anyway."

"That's something you know, of course, but a thief wouldn't. Or they might've thought your daughter had some valuable electronics. But don't worry, ma'am. We're going to investigate and let you know as soon as we know more."

"Thank you," my mom said.

"Melody, what do you think? Is there anyone who might be targeting you for another prank? Anyone who might want something from your room?" Rhys' father studied me closely.

Like your son?

But even though I was pissed off at the boys, I knew telling Rhys' father anything about it would be a mistake.

Even if I could use the emails I'd exchanged with the boys as some kind of proof—even though it would be incomplete because they hadn't admitted anything—that the boys definitely had a problem with me, I didn't think Rhys' father was the one who'd help me.

He'd probably only blow up at Rhys, and yeah, maybe I should just let Rhys deal with the consequences of what he and his friends had done, but I couldn't do it.

Knowing Rhys' father, things could go too far.

"I don't know," I finally said.

"Okay. If you notice anything's missing, you let me know, all right?"

"Yeah." But I already knew that nothing was missing.

They hadn't come here to steal my things. At least not this time.

And I didn't have any money just lying around. Maybe if they'd had more time, they would've taken something.

Ugh.

I still couldn't believe they'd do something like this.

As I looked around at the mess that was my room, I almost wanted revenge too.

Why were they doing this to me? Since they hadn't found anything, had they finally realized I was innocent?

My phone still hadn't vibrated with the text that contained their apology, so I supposed that the answer was *no*.

CHAPTER 9

I t took me hours to sort through all the stuff in my room. When I was done, I threw myself on my bed and groaned, sweat beading my forehead.

"Honey," my mom said as she stepped through the open door. "There's going to be a police car just down the street watching our neighborhood for a few days. It's only to make sure that no one else breaks in and tries anything, okay?"

"Yeah." I wasn't afraid that the boys would return.

They hadn't found what they were looking for here.

What was going to be next? My locker? I'd have to make sure I wasn't alone at all. Not even on my way to school and back.

"Are you all right? If you don't feel safe here, maybe we can go—"

"It's fine, Mom. Don't worry." I managed to flash her a smile. "But if you don't feel safe here—"

"No. I'm perfectly fine with being here. Our house is safe. I checked all the windows, and the front and back doors are locked. Your dad is going to sleep in the living room tonight, so if anyone tries to get in, they're going to regret it." The corners of her lips lifted up.

"Great. I'm so tired."

"Then get some sleep."

I fully intended to do that, but first I had to call Sam and make sure that I wouldn't be alone tomorrow.

When my mom closed the door, I grabbed my phone.

Sam answered almost immediately.

"Oh, my god! I was just about to call you," she blurted out. "I can't believe this. It's crazy, right?"

"Probably, but I'm not sure what you're talking about." Had she somehow found out what the boys had done?

I doubted it, which meant there was something else. Ah, wonderful.

Just what I needed.

The beginning of a headache pressed on my temples. Would this shit ever end?

"The Ember High Journal? Wait, if you don't know, then what did you want to tell me?" Surprised filled her voice.

Of course it had to be that damn website again. Everything was always about it.

"I haven't had the chance to check it because I've been cleaning up my room. After *someone*," I emphasized the word so she'd know who I was talking about, "basically ransacked it to try to find something I can't possibly have."

"Oh, my god! Are you okay?!"

"Yeah. Nothing was taken, but they made a huge mess. Broke my lamp too."

"Did you tell the cops about—"

"Not exactly. I mean, it's not like I have any proof. And you know who showed up at my door? The *only* cop in town." I rolled my eyes, even though she couldn't see me.

"Rhys' dad?"

"Who else?" I muttered.

"Shit. What did he say? Is he protecting Rhys?"

"I don't think he knows anything. The cops were checking out my house, but they didn't really find anything. I don't think they'll catch anyone." It wasn't like the boys regularly broke into people's houses.

No one would ever suspect them, even if they'd been spotted in the area. Sure, they didn't mind stealing people's money and lunch at school, but that wasn't quite the same, and no one had ever reported any of it.

"You could've told them and seen what they'd do, even if it turned out to be nothing," Sam said. "Aren't you at least curious? Sure, we both expect they'd just tell us we're crazy and imagining things, but what if we're wrong? What if they'd believe you?"

"Rhys' father would lose his mind. I don't think we want that. But enough about that. What's up with our *favorite* website?"

"Um."

"Oh, come on. Do I have to turn on my laptop again and go check for myself?"

"Okay, I'll tell you. There are two new posts, and they're both about our four idiots."

"What? Are you kidding me?"

"Apparently, the rumors weren't enough, so now some proof was posted too. For those who didn't believe it, I guess."

"What proof?" I sat up, suddenly no longer feeling tired.

"Well, it's nothing too weird or anything, but there are some blurry photos of Ethan actually holding a syringe and taking steroids, I guess. Then Aaron switching urine cups with Rhys right outside the bathroom when they thought no one could see them. Then a few pics of Zack's empty living room and kitchen. And one very blurry photo of Rhys leaning on the window with what looks like blood on his face. You can see it for yourself. But that's not all."

"There's more?"

"Yeah. There's a post saying that all four guys are in love with you."

My mouth fell open. "What? No!"

"That's what it says. There's no proof, though. But the post is getting a lot of attention."

"What the fuck? Why would someone post that?" I supposed someone could've seen me kissing the boys at the party, but why post about it now?

"To mess with our bullies even more, because obviously the first round wasn't enough."

"I know, but it's like that person knows everything about them. And now they'll think I did it to get revenge because they," I lowered my voice, "ransacked my room."

"Yeah, the timing was kind of terrible."

I couldn't help but wonder if that person was actually following the boys. Maybe they even had proof of the boys getting inside my house.

But who were they? Did I know them?

"Any idea who could've taken those pics?" I asked.

"Nope. Not a clue. But I think this person, whoever they are, is actually worse than Rhys. They're not just posting stuff people submit. I think they're a stalker too."

"Maybe more students banded together, and they're trying to expose the bullies."

"I don't know. I think the photos were taken with the same device. Probably just one person. You have to take a look and tell me what you see."

"I will. But we also need a plan. I can't be alone at school. Not in the hallway, and not in the bathroom or the library, or anywhere, really. If the guys corner me again, I don't know what they're going to do to me."

"Don't worry. I'll come pick you up tomorrow morning, and we'll go to school together. I won't leave your side, even if I'm late for class, and you should stay somewhere with lots of people until I can get to you. I'll ask Keith if he's willing to help too."

"Thanks. I feel like I should hire a bodyguard or something."

"I'll be your bodyguard. You need at least one. I still think you should tell someone about what's going on. Maybe report it anonymously or something. Now that your name's on that website along with theirs, it won't seem so outlandish that they might be after you."

"I'll think about it." I needed to do something.

Things had already gotten way too out of hand. The boys were like a pack of hungry wolves, and they didn't care who they ripped apart.

CHAPTER 10

"Are you out of your mind?" Sam gaped at me after I told her the plan I'd come up with during school. "I don't think that's a good idea. What makes you think they'll change their minds when you tried it like a billion times already, and all that happened was that they got even worse?"

"I've been thinking. They're like a pack of wolves. When they're together, it's hard to even talk to them because there are too many of them. Too many voices yelling over mine. But if I can talk to them one-on-one in relative safety, somewhere they can't do anything to hurt me, then maybe I can get them to stand down, or at least to tell me who could've taken those photos of them."

"Um, like I said, it's an incredibly stupid plan. You

already tried it with Rhys, and he yelled at you and told you to leave. Why do you think this time will be different?"

"Well, Rhys was... He was upset because his father was there, and he was cuffed to the bed. Of course he wasn't willing to talk to me. It was humiliating and distressing for him."

"So you're still trying to make excuses for them. Great." Sam crossed her arms.

I bit down on my lip. "Maybe. A little. But how else am I going to stop them? I mean, I could go to someone and maybe hope they'd take action, but what if that only makes things worse and we don't figure out who owns the website now? And what if the boys only get angrier at me? I can't walk around with bodyguards all the time as if I'm the president or something."

"You know what I think?" She pressed her lips into a tight line.

"What?"

"I think you like them. Like really like them. And even though you try to be reasonable, you can't because you keep hoping you'll get whatever you shared with them back."

I just stared at her.

Yeah, there was probably some truth to that.

I did miss them. I missed being around them, getting to know them, and just hanging out.

"Don't try to deny it," Sam said. "I know they're hot. I'm not blind, you know. But you shouldn't put yourself at risk for them, or do anything for them. They can get themselves out of their own mess. You don't have to help them."

"I'm not going to help—"

"If you find whoever has the password, you will be helping them. I know it's important to stop that person, but you don't need those four bullies for that."

"But we have nothing. No info or anything. What if one of them knows something? What if they've seen someone and just can't be bothered to try to remember it? What if I could help them remember, and then we all get what we want?"

"Okay, fine." She made a show of stepping aside. Aaron's house was right behind her. "Go talk to Aaron and see how it goes."

I eyed the house for a few moments.

Aaron was supposed to be home right now, and his parents too. If I went to see him, him kicking me out was the worst thing that could happen.

He wouldn't do anything to me in front of his parents.

I took a deep breath and took a step forward,

which made Sam huff. But I didn't want to give up on my plan, so I strode to the front door and rang the bell.

Aaron's mom opened the door a few moments later.

"Hi, Mrs. Oliveira," I said with my sweetest smile. "I'm here to see Aaron. We have a project for school that we need to do."

"Oh, okay. Come in." She opened the door wider and I entered. "He's in his room."

"Thanks." I flashed her another smile and headed to Aaron's room.

I knocked on his door, bracing myself.

"What?" he snapped, and I pushed the door open.

"Hey," I said softly.

Aaron was sitting on the floor, his back resting against the bed, his knees drawn up. When his head turned to me, his eyes filled with anger.

"What the fuck are you doing here?" He sprang to his feet.

"I just want to talk, okay?"

"No, it's not okay." His stomach rumbled, and his jaw clenched. "Just leave. I don't want to talk to you."

I reached into my bag and pulled out a candy bar, offering it to him.

He scoffed, and I thought he was going to turn away from me, but instead, he snatched the candy bar.

"I just want a few minutes of your time. That's all," I said.

He tore the wrapper in a second and stuffed the candy bar into his mouth. "Then start talking."

"I already said I don't control the Journal for like a billion times, so I'm not going to repeat it. But it should be obvious I'm not the one you're looking for. Why would I do any of that? You pissed off a lot of people. Do you really think no one else would want to take you down? Someone else could've gotten into Rhys' room."

"It was you."

"How do you know? Was there a camera in Rhys' room? Wait, don't answer that. I already know the answer. There isn't. Because then you'd know it wasn't me."

"Oh, come on. Everyone's just crazy to break into a cop's house. You know things about us. We let you get close. Too close."

"Really? We were working on our project. Or do you think I somehow arranged that too so I could get close to you? Just forget your anger for a second and think. It doesn't make any sense for me to be doing any of that. And I definitely don't want to be part of school gossip, and I would never want to ruin other people's lives by posting shit online about them. Didn't you see those photos that were posted? Someone was stalking you and probably has been doing it for a while. Maybe you saw that person, but you didn't pay enough attention because you thought you were untouchable."

"Someone like you? Because you could've been around us and our houses all the time. If anyone saw you, you could've just told them you were there because of the project, and everyone would've believed you and forgotten they'd even seen you. You can pass around unseen because no one thinks you're a threat."

"Wow, am I a super-spy now or something? Why do you want me to be guilty so much? I don't get it. It's not like I did anything to you. Actually, you did it to me, remember?"

He just kept looking at me, and there was something in his eyes that I couldn't identify.

"Have you taken a closer look at the photos? There might be something in them that can help you remember who was around you, especially the photos taken in the boys' locker room."

He grabbed his laptop and opened it. "You want me to look at the photos again? Fine."

I approached as he set the laptop on the bed. Sitting down on the edge of the bed, I glanced at Aaron, who settled not too far away from me.

His mouth opened as his gaze kept lifting to me, but then he brought up the Journal in his browser.

"Tell me what I'm looking for," he said.

I leaned forward, my arm nearly brushing against his. "Focus on every detail in the photos."

"They're shit quality."

"Yeah, but that doesn't mean there isn't anything useful."

He sighed. "Okay."

"Do you remember when this might've been taken?" I asked, clicking on one of the photos.

"I don't know. It could've been after practice."

"Was there someone in the locker room with you?"

"There wasn't supposed to be. I checked everything before—"

"What about a hidden camera? Someone could've set it up somewhere."

"I haven't seen anything."

"Wait." I furrowed my brow as I took a closer look at one of the photos. "Isn't that—"

Aaron leaned forward, his shoulder pressing against mine. The contact sent a current of electricity through me, and our gazes met before we both focused on the photo again.

"That's you," he said.

I was a blurry shape behind Rhys, but it was definitely me. "It has to be from that time when he told me to come with him to keep watch."

"Just because you're in the photo doesn't prove anything," Aaron said, but he didn't sound all that convinced now. "You could've had help."

"Ah, so now there's a bunch of people involved. Is it so hard to accept that it wasn't me?" I eyed him carefully.

His eyes were trained on mine, and for a second, I got lost in them and forgot why I was even here. It would be so easy to close the distance between us and brush my lips against his.

"You should go," he said quietly, his voice hoarse.

"Yeah, I guess I should." I hopped to my feet and glanced back at him before going through the door.

Maybe, just maybe, I could get through to my boys.

CHAPTER 11

Encouraged by my tiny progress, I decided to pay Rhys another visit too.

Now that he was going to school again, maybe things would be a bit better. But it wasn't only that. I'd overheard that the cops were needed because of some hostage situation, so I hoped Rhys' father would be away.

But when I was about to ring the doorbell, I heard noises.

Shouting.

Rhys' father was definitely home. Fuck.

I should leave, but I didn't want to leave Rhys when I knew he was in trouble, so I pressed the doorbell anyway.

A few moments later, the noise completely died down. Rhys' father opened the door. He reeked of alcohol and his eyes were bloodshot, but he put on his charming smile in an instant.

"Melody. What are you doing here so late?" he asked.

"Um, sorry. But just as I was about to submit the project Rhys and I are working on and that's due today, I realized we made a mistake, and we need to fix it ASAP." Behind him, I could see Rhys just standing there and looking at me with wide eyes.

"Ah," his father said.

"Is Rhys here? If this isn't a good time, I—"

"He is. Come in."

I stepped inside. "Hey," I said to Rhys. "We totally messed up the last part of our project. I misread the last question and I realized it when I was rereading it."

"Right." Rhys licked his lips, glancing at his father.

"Can we go to your room or do you want to do it somewhere else?" I asked.

If he wanted to get out of the house, we could just talk somewhere else. Some crowded place.

"Um, my room."

"Rhys," his father called. "Come here for a sec."

I hesitated as Rhys approached his father, who was standing on the opposite end of the room.

Rhys' father caught his son's arm and whispered something into his ear. It would've almost looked affectionate if I couldn't see Rhys' tense jaw.

His father let him go then, clapping him on the back and laughing softly.

Rhys strode toward me, and when we were in his room, he leaned against the door and closed his eyes for a moment. When he opened them, he was glaring at me.

"What the fuck are you doing here?" he hissed.

"If you want me to leave, I will. But I just want to talk."

"There's nothing to talk about."

"Really? Have you talked to Aaron? There's a chance someone is stalking not just you, but all of us. You can't know who was in your room. Maybe there's something that can help us figure that out. Some kind of clue or something. Did you leave the window open? Your computer on?"

"I know you're in one of the pics, but that doesn't mean anything."

I let out a frustrated groan. "Okay, fine. Then I'm leaving."

"No!" Rhys got in my way before I could open the door. "No. You can't go."

"Can we talk then?"

"Yeah, whatever. Talk."

"I don't know why you think it's all my fault."

"You used my computer and logged in."

"Yeah, a fact we all know already. But the password wasn't changed then, was it? Why do you think I'd wait? Did you have the password written down somewhere? Because I don't think you did, and even if you did, you'd be able to tell if the file containing it was open. And if it was just jotted down in one of your notebooks, how the hell would I even find it? I don't think you're stupid. Someone had to have changed the password through your computer if you left it on while we were at the party. I guess you left your email open too, so it wasn't hard for someone to reset the password through it, if the Journal functions like most websites."

"You ran from the party and got here, and changed my password."

"Why? Why wouldn't I just change it the first time?"

"Because I'd know it was you for sure."

"So I just got up and left, hoping that I'd get another chance? Please. That sounds impossible. I couldn't have known you'd leave your window open, or your computer on, or whatever the hell it was that you think I did. How could I have planned all that?"

"Then what do you say happened?"

"Obviously, I wasn't involved in any way. You did whatever you did and left for the party. Someone has been watching you for a while, so they were watching then too, and figured out they had a way in and could access your computer. They opened the website and figured out they were logged in as the admin, so they changed the password and happily ran off."

"And who did it?" He pressed his lips into a tight line.

"How should I know?" I made my way to the windows. "So, was a window open or not?"

"It was. My mom probably opened it. That one." He pointed at it.

I eyed the window. "Huh. Looks a bit high. How on earth would I climb in and out unseen? If I was a tall, skinny person who could easily climb anything, then maybe yeah."

Rhys mumbled something under his breath.

"Are you the only one who had the password? What if Ethan, Zack, or Aaron accidentally logged in somewhere and forgot about it?" I glanced over my shoulder at him.

"No, it was only me. We thought my house was the safest because no one would want to get anywhere near my dad. And even if someone figured it out or accused me of running the website, my dad would make sure the whole thing went away and no one knew anything. No one would just get a search warrant for our house based on a rumor without him knowing about it before it even happened."

I frowned.

That all made sense, but it was also a huge risk for Rhys. Even if his father was willing to cover up things, Rhys would be in a whole lot of trouble.

"Okay, so someone had to have gotten inside this room," I said. "I guess that narrows our search a bit."

Just as I was about to turn around, something colorful caught my eye. I bent down to pick it up. It was a small sticker with a cute red dinosaur on it.

"What's this?" I asked, turning to Rhys.

He got closer, his frown deepening. "That's not mine."

"Then whose could it be? Did you have any guests in the house recently? Someone who could've snuck into your room when no one was watching?"

He shook his head. "No one was here, except you."

"And you didn't see this thing before? Have you even looked for any clues?"

"Oh, yeah, I had plenty of time for that while my dad was—" He bit down on his lip.

"Fine, you haven't seen it. But now we have a clue, and please don't tell me I dropped it here right now because I know you've been watching me like a hawk, and I couldn't have just produced this sticker out of thin air. If it were mine, I would've just collected it and told you nothing."

"It's just a dumb sticker."

"But it might be a clue."

"Yeah right."

"Then I'll take it." I didn't know if the sticker would help or not.

Maybe it was just a dumb thing Rhys didn't remember getting or it had somehow slipped between his things and he'd unknowingly brought it here.

But maybe it was more.

The thief could've dropped it too, especially if they were in a hurry or hadn't planned on getting inside Rhys' house. It would've been difficult to plan such a thing anyway, so they must've been on the lookout for a while.

"Whatever," Rhys said.

"I need to go now." It was getting very late already.

"Okay, but give me a moment." Rhys quietly opened the door and slipped outside. "Let's go," he whispered to me. "Just be very quiet."

I padded after him.

Through an open door, I could see his father asleep in an armchair. Hopefully, he wouldn't wake.

Rhys opened the front door for me, and before I left, I glanced at him.

Our gazes locked for a few moments, and his lips parted as if he was about to say something, but he didn't.

I tightly held the sticker in my hand.

More progress.

CHAPTER 12

When I found out that Ethan had applied for an essay writing competition, I thought I knew where I could find him if I wanted to talk to him alone.

He'd probably be at the library, and the rest of the boys wouldn't be with him because he'd want to be able to fully focus on his task.

Actually, the writing competition had to be very important to him. As I was checking out the history of the competition and the list of winners, I found his brother's name.

Winning would mean a whole lot for Ethan. Maybe bothering him wasn't the best choice, but he wouldn't yell at me in the middle of the library if he didn't want to get kicked out. Or at least I hoped he wouldn't.

Besides, the boys must've talked, and if by now they didn't have any doubts about me being guilty, then they were truly idiots.

"Where are you going?" Sam asked as I started in the direction of the school library.

"Library," I said. "You don't have to come with me. I'll be fine."

There were plenty of people in the hallways, and the library was safe too. If Ethan cared about the competition, he wouldn't have the time to bully me.

"Are you sure?" Sam asked.

"Yeah. I'll text you later."

"Okay." She headed in the opposite direction.

When I got to the library, I spotted Ethan as he was frowning at one of the shelves.

"What are you looking for? Maybe I can help you," I said.

He narrowed his eyes at me. "I don't need your help."

After snatching a book, he headed for one of the tables. His notebook and pens were already all out and ready on the table.

I sat in the empty chair across from him.

His gaze lifted to me. "There are other tables. You can sit there. I'm busy."

"Are you working on your essay?" I tilted my head.

"Maybe I can help you brainstorm, or I can proofread it for you."

"Why? So you can steal my idea too?" He kept his voice low as he leaned forward in his chair. "Isn't it enough that you got me kicked off the football team?"

"Um, I don't think I was the one using steroids. You're really good at football. I don't know why you were even using that shit. And I know even less why you keep insisting that I spilled your secret."

"Fuck off." He lowered his gaze to his notebook and picked up his pen.

Okay, if he wanted to be like that, then I could just wait. I reached into my bag and pulled out a book.

Ethan glanced at me a few times as I read my book.

After a few minutes, he tore a piece of paper out of his notebook, crumpled it in his fingers and threw it across the table.

The paper fell on the floor not too far away from me, and I took it, opening it. After reading through what he'd written, I looked up at him.

"This is really good, actually," I said.

"What do you know?" he snapped.

"But you should switch this paragraph with the last one." I pointed at it.

His brow furrowed, and he pushed himself up to

grab the paper from me. He looked at it for a while and then mumbled something under his breath.

"What did you say?" I asked.

"You're right," he said through his teeth. "But it's never going to be as good as Roan's. All I can hope for is that someone reads the damn thing without laughing."

"Why do you do that to yourself?"

His eyes met mine. "Do what?"

"Keep thinking that you're not good enough and that anything you do can't possibly be up to standard or a winning piece."

"You obviously haven't seen me fail at pretty much everything I try." He sighed.

"Actually, no. Our project was a success. You won football games. You're not failing all your classes."

"Not failing doesn't mean you're exceptional either."

"No one's exceptional at everything."

"My brother is."

"I bet he's not," I said. "You just think he is."

"Why are you doing this? Do you think that if you make me feel better, I'm going to believe anything you say?"

I shrugged. "I'm not the one who wants to ruin your life or make things more difficult for you. Someone else is. I just want to find them because you're not the only one whose life they're ruining. Have you seen anyone acting weird around you? Anyone watching you closer than they should?"

"In case you haven't noticed, everyone watches me." He turned his head in the direction of a girl who was gawking at him from across the room.

Okay, he had a point.

Despite everything, the boys were still the hottest people in our school. Everyone was going to watch them, and now everyone was even more interested in what they were doing because of what had happened.

"Can you leave me to finish this crap in peace?" he asked.

"Sure, but it's not crap." I gave him a small smile, and then stuffed my book into my bag and got to my feet. "Good luck, Ethan."

He muttered *thanks* under his breath.

CHAPTER 13

"Was that Ethan?" Sam asked when she met me in front of the library.

"Yeah."

"So you went to the library to talk to him? Are you still trying to get them back on your side? Because, really, if anyone should be begging, it's them, not you. They don't deserve you." Her face was serious.

"I know what you think, and yeah, I know it's not ideal. But I really want this whole thing to clear up. I don't want them to hate me forever." I supposed it sounded pathetic, like I was some lovesick girl who just couldn't accept that the guy, or guys, she liked didn't like her back and treated her like shit.

And maybe I was.

Those tiny glimpses with the boys that reminded me

of how things had been between us before all the drama made me believe that there was still something left worth fighting for.

"Whatever you say, but I really think you should just forget about ever being friends with them again. They're assholes. Even if you fix things, who says they won't jump on you the next time some shit happens? They have their little group already, and they won't take any new members."

Sam and I headed home, but when we reached a small park not too far away from our school, I spotted Zack sitting on one of the benches.

It looked like he was waiting for someone, because when one of the boys from our school appeared in view, Zack got to his feet.

I recognized the boy. Zack used to torment him and steal his money. Shit.

"Sam, can you give me a moment?" I asked.

She followed my gaze and groaned. "How am I supposed to keep you safe from those assholes when you actively look for them? I don't get it."

"It'll be fine. I promise. I just need to do something." I dashed toward Zack because he was already on his way to the boy.

"Hey." I got in Zack's way.

He was about to sidestep me, so I placed my hand on

his arm.

"What do you want? Money or food?" I asked, a shudder running through my hand at the contact.

His lips parted, his eyes widening slightly. "I don't know what you're talking about."

"Oh, come on. You were going for that guy to steal something from him. Don't deny it." I glanced over my shoulder.

The boy had spotted Zack and me and was now quickly getting away from us. Relief flooded me, and I let my hand drop to my side.

"I— Did you come here to mock me or what?" Zack asked.

"No, I didn't. I just came here to stop you from doing something you shouldn't be doing. You're better than this. I know it, and probably, deep down, you know it too."

He just watched me in silence.

"Look, I know your parents didn't want you to get a job before, but now you're on your own, right? You could get a job. Or you can reach out to someone for help. There are so many things you can do that don't include terrorizing others."

"What's your game?" he asked. "What are you trying to achieve?"

"There's no game. All I want is to stop bullies. And

the person who's now running that website is a bully."

"Does that mean I'm a bully too?" He cocked his head, his eyes trained on mine.

"I'm pretty sure you know the answer to that. You're not dumb, Zack." I turned on my heel and walked away from him.

Sam was waiting for me, and I didn't want to waste any more of her time.

"What happened?" she asked as soon as I reached her.

"Not much. But I'm starting to think that Zack's, Ethan's, Rhys', and Aaron's lives flipped upside down when all that stuff was posted and they just don't know how to handle it. It's like they had this system that was totally messed up but was working, and now they know nothing anymore. It has to be scary, and they're lashing out at me because they don't know what else to do."

Sam's eyebrows arched. "Wow, since when did you become a bully psychologist?"

"I didn't, but maybe I just got an idea what college I'll pick." Figuring out what people thought and how they behaved and why seemed interesting.

I wished I could know what was going on in my boys' heads because I sure like hell didn't know what was going on in mine.

Maybe we were all just confused.

And a little bit lost.

CHAPTER 14

I agreed to meet with Sam at school because I thought that I'd made some progress with the boys and that they'd think a little before jumping me for no good reason.

But as I strode through the school hallway full of people, I had a feeling like someone was watching me. Whenever I looked in the direction of the sensation, I couldn't see anyone, so I thought that I was just being paranoid and imagining it.

But when I spun around faster than before, I caught a glimpse of Rhys.

He quickly ducked behind a wall, but I was sure it was him and that he'd been watching me.

Okay, maybe I was wrong about the boys. It wouldn't

be the first time I'd completely misjudged their thought process.

I quickened my steps and breathed out a sigh of relief when I spotted Sam and Keith.

"Hey, guys," I said, and they both smiled at me.

"Are you okay?" Sam's brow furrowed a moment later as if she could tell I was still tense.

"Yeah."

"Did you see the new post?" Sam asked.

I blinked at her. "The Journal again?"

She nodded. "But don't worry. It's not about you."

"Okay." That was a relief. "Then what does it say?"

"It looks like someone broke into one girl's locker. Her name's Ashley. The creep—I'm just gonna call them that because we still don't know who they are and they're creepy as fuck—somehow figured out that Ashley has a social media account where she pretends she's like twenty-one or something. And she posted a ton of sexy pics. Really sexy ones. The pics are now all over the Journal."

I gasped. I didn't know Ashley, but that was horrible, and it only confirmed that the new admin of the Journal wasn't a nice person.

"You can imagine how Ashley's doing. Everyone's saying terrible things to her, so her mom had to come pick her up because she couldn't stay at school," Sam said.

"It's disgusting," Keith said. "The school hasn't done anything about the Journal. I don't think they're even trying to figure out who's behind it. And I won't even mention the cops. They're useless."

"Is there anything we could do?" I asked. "I mean, I know we haven't come up with any ideas, and if the cops don't know where to start, then we're going to have even less luck."

"Maybe we should set up a trap for the creep," Keith said.

"What kind of trap?" I focused on him.

"I don't know. Maybe we can pretend we have some super-secret information that everyone will want to know, and we can hide it in one of the lockers. And then we wait to see who shows up."

"It's not a bad idea, but I doubt it'll work," Sam said. "We can't watch a locker all day. It would be impossible."

"We can hide a camera inside the locker," Keith said. "So when the creep opens it, we'll see them."

"But what if the creep sends someone else to do it? The website still accepts submissions, so maybe the creep wasn't the one who figured out Ashley's account. They could've gotten it from someone else's and just posted it. And now that they know everyone's secrets, they could blackmail anyone into doing anything they want, and we'd end up with the wrong person," I said.

"Dammit," Keith said. "I haven't really thought about that, but maybe it would be a good start. We catch one person, then get some info out of them. And eventually, we get to the creep."

"We could do that, but we could also get in trouble," Sam said. "And I have an important exam this week. I don't really have the time to chase after some creep."

"We can come up with something else," Keith said. "Next week, then?"

"Sure," Sam said, and I nodded.

Coming up with a decent plan that wouldn't get us in trouble too or make us lose too much precious time that we didn't have if we wanted to pass our exams wasn't going to be easy, but maybe together we could figure it out.

CHAPTER 15

When I got a text from the boys after school, I stared at it for a full minute. They'd invited me to come meet them. All four of them at the same time.

I wasn't sure if it was a trap or if they'd finally seen reason and stopped blaming me for all their problems. But I really wanted to find out.

If I told Sam to come with me, I didn't think the boys would want to talk to me, and she would probably think I was doing the stupidest thing ever.

But maybe there was another way. I could ask them to meet me at a crowded restaurant or some other safe place where they couldn't do anything to me because there'd be plenty of witnesses.

My mom could take me there, so there'd be no risk

for me on my way there and back. Rhys had been following me, and I had no idea why. If they thought they could trick me, they were wrong.

I texted them back and waited for their answer. When they agreed, hope simmered inside me, and I was instantly angry with myself because of it.

Why was I still hoping we could mend things between us? Why was I hoping we could be friends or maybe even more?

It was crazy, and I didn't even know if I should forgive them. Of course, as I was thinking that, I was already getting ready and wondering what I should wear.

As if it mattered.

Except it did.

I wanted to look nice for them, and that pissed me off even more. I put the blouse I was holding back into my closet. I should stop thinking about what they might like and just pick something I knew I'd like.

Once I finally settled on a dark red shirt and black pants, I got dressed. But then I got another idea. I might not really need Sam to protect me, but there was something else that might be useful, so I dialed her number.

"Hey, what's up?" she said when she answered.

"Do you have some free time? I'm going to meet with

Ethan, Zack, Rhys, and Aaron, and before you say anything, don't worry. We're meeting at the most public place in our town and my mom's taking me there. But if you're free, then maybe you could be close by. Just in case our creep or someone else shows up. I mean, if they're following the boys, they'll probably want to know what they're up to now."

"Oh! You want me to stalk the stalker? Yep, I have time for that! And that doesn't mean I won't have time to keep an eye on you too."

"Great!" I gave her all the details.

Maybe we could get closer to figuring out who was behind this mess.

MY STOMACH WAS FULL OF BUTTERFLIES WHEN I ENTERED the restaurant.

A part of me expected someone to jump out and throw something in my face. Maybe another stupid trick from the boys, but one that would humiliate me in front of the whole town and not just the school.

But when I saw them at the table across from me, I felt a bit better. At least I wouldn't have to wait for them.

They all looked up at me, and I could feel their eyes scanning me up and down.

"Hey," I said as I took a seat in the only empty chair.

"We didn't know if you'd come," Aaron said, almost shyly.

"Well, I'm here now. So what is that you wanted to tell me?" I eyed them carefully.

"We wanted to say that we're sorry," Ethan said. "For what we did and said to you."

"Okay." Hearing the apology sounded good, but it would mean nothing until they proved that they were really sorry and not just playing me to get whatever they wanted.

"We were wrong," Rhys said.

"What changed your minds?" I asked.

"We followed you," Rhys said, and my eyebrows shot up.

It had been all of them?

Ah shit.

"Why?" I crossed my arms, glaring at them.

"We just wanted to make sure that it wasn't you," Aaron said. "The website was updated when you weren't on your phone or near any computers, and we know that an update can't be scheduled."

"Right," I said. "But you don't think anymore that I have helpers?"

"You would never have posted that stuff about

Ashley," Zack said, his eyes meeting mine. "Even if you just wanted to play us."

"Wow, so you know that much about me. Nice." I wasn't too impressed, but I supposed I should be glad we were over the part where they only blamed me.

"Can you forgive us?" Rhys asked.

"I'll think about that. Is that all you wanted to say to me?"

"Actually, no." Aaron scratched the back of his head. "We came up with a plan to figure out who has access to the website, and we need your help."

"What kind of plan?" I tilted my head.

"You can't tell anyone about it, not even the people you trust most. It would only be among the five of us and no one more. Not even your bestie," Aaron said.

"Okay, I guess. I can keep a secret. You don't have to worry about that. But what's the plan?" I wasn't about to do anything crazy or stupid that could get me in trouble.

Despite everything the boys had just said, I couldn't lower my guard around them. This could all still be some kind of trap for me.

"We're still coming up with the details," Ethan said. "We just need to know if we can count on you or not."

I chewed on the inside of my cheek. "Okay, but I'll only do it if I'm comfortable with it. I'm not going to go along with some insane plan."

The boys exchanged a few glances.

"Okay," Aaron said. "Thanks."

"Now that we have a deal, we should order some food," Zack said. "I'm starving."

I liked his plan very much.

❧

When I got out of the restaurant, I immediately spotted Sam, who was watching me with a suspicious look on her face.

I had a bag full of food in my hand, and I offered it to her.

"Thanks for doing this for me. The least I could do is get you some food. You should try this stuff. It's delicious," I said.

"Thanks." She took the bag. "But tell me about the important stuff. What did they want?"

"They apologized, and then we had lunch. We talked about random stuff, like school." I shrugged. "It was nice, actually."

"Just that?" She raised an eyebrow at me.

"Yeah." The boys had asked me not to tell anyone about their plan in the making, so I wasn't going to tell Sam either.

There was no need for her to know at the moment

anyway.

"And you actually forgave them?" she asked.

"Not yet."

"So they invite you to lunch, say they're sorry, and they're your friends again?"

"I don't know. We'll see. But it's a step in a good direction, right?"

She pressed her lips into a tight line.

"Have you seen anyone from our school? Or anyone acting weird?"

She shook her head. "I think everyone was here just to get lunch. Maybe the creep isn't always following someone. I mean, they probably have a life too. They need to do homework and stuff."

"True. But it was worth a shot."

"Yeah. Too bad it didn't work." She opened the bag with food. "Oh, my god. You're right. This smells absolutely amazing."

I looked around, but I couldn't see anyone familiar either. It was going to be a problem if the creep was an ex-student because then we might not recognize them.

But for now, I was happy.

The boys were no longer after me. I had a feeling that they weren't faking the whole thing.

Hopefully, I wasn't being delusional.

I got woken up by a text.

It was from Sam.

As I squinted at the text, my heart leaped into my throat. Sam wanted me to check the Journal because the newest post was all about me.

I was immediately wide-awake and groaned in frustration when the internet browser on my phone took too long to open.

When I saw the Journal's front page, I felt lightheaded. There was an image of me, and then a few images of me going to the restaurant, and even a few pics of the boys and me together at our table.

They were blurry again, but I was sure they'd been taken from somewhere outside the restaurant, through one of the windows.

We would've seen if someone had been taking photos of us, and there was definitely something in the way, like a glass surface.

Sam swore that she hadn't seen anyone, and she had no clue how the pics could've been taken. My gaze lowered to the text under the photos.

The most wanted girl in school: Melody Reid

The creep claimed that Ethan, Zack, Aaron, and Rhys were all trying to date me because, apparently, they weren't so popular anymore, so they had to settle for less, meaning me.

Ugh!

That was just ridiculous.

The creep said the boys would have to fight it out. And the comments on the post... I didn't even want to look at them, but I couldn't turn my head away either.

They were brutal.

Some people called me a slut and a whore who was playing four guys at the same time. Others laughed at the boys for having to date someone like me instead of one of the popular, pretty girls. Some were offering themselves to the boys because they were a better choice.

I took a deep breath and closed the website.

This was so much bullshit. But who had taken those

photos? And how come Sam hadn't seen them or recognized them?

It was possible they'd been very careful, and maybe it really was someone we didn't know all that well.

We couldn't know or recognize every single student at our school. But maybe the creep had simply hired someone. That way there was no risk we'd figure them out.

My phone rang a few moments later. Aaron's number was on the screen.

"Hello?" I said and cleared my dry throat.

"Mel?" Aaron said. "Have you seen—"

"Yep."

"We're all here," he said. "And we have a plan."

"Okay. Tell me."

"We think we can use this situation in our favor."

"How?" I wasn't looking forward to having everyone laugh and giggle at me at school.

"The creep probably wants attention, and any post about us is going to get it. We're going to be the only thing everyone will talk about, so maybe we can give them some more material."

"What?" I couldn't see how that was a good plan.

"The creep needs more material to write more posts. We can give it to them, but we can also set up a trap."

"And how would that work?"

"We'd go on a date. I mean, you'd go on a date with all of us. Separately, one by one. We would make it seem like you were meeting us in secret. While you're on a date with one of us, the rest would be close by, watching everything. If the creep or someone else shows up, we catch them. Either we get the one we're looking for, or we get someone who can lead us to them."

I thought about it for a few moments. Going on dates with my boys?

Well, that sounded... interesting.

"Are you sure we can make it work? I mean, what if no one can recognize this person? What if it's someone who's no longer a student at our school?"

"If they want revenge on us, then one of us has to know them, even if their face is just vaguely familiar to us. And we can see if someone's taking photos," Aaron said.

"Do you even remember all your victims?" I asked.

There was a brief silence on the other end of the line.

"I think so, yeah," Aaron said.

"Okay. But what if other students get involved? Someone might want to brag they're the one who submitted the photos or something."

"The photos were taken with the same device."

"How do you know?" I asked.

"Rhys figured it out. There was some info that wasn't completely deleted."

"Okay. But there's a chance the creep hired someone so we wouldn't know who it was."

"True, but we can still catch that person. If there's money involved, then they have to know who's paying them. Or at least have an account or contact info that we can use to get to the creep."

"All right. I'm in."

"Awesome," Aaron said. "We're going to text you more details, but don't forget that no one's supposed to know about this. You're not supposed to tell anyone where you're going when you meet with us. If anyone asks, just invent something."

"Okay, I guess." We'd find out soon enough how our plan would turn out.

CHAPTER 17

My first fake date was with Zack.

I was supposed to meet him at the park. Maybe if Ethan, Aaron, and Rhys were watching our every step, then hopefully we could catch the creep.

The boys had picked the park because it was the best place with enough hiding spots for them, but Zack and I would still be in open view. They'd planned everything we were supposed to do, but they haven't given me all the details.

As soon as I spotted Zack, my stomach did a nervous flip. He stood next to an empty bench, his hands in the pockets of his jacket as if he didn't know what to do with them.

"Hey," I said with a small smile, and even my voice sounded lame to me.

"Hey." He smiled back.

"How are we going to do this? Am I supposed to hug you or something?" I asked.

He looked around. "I don't see anyone. Maybe we can just take a walk first. We don't know if the creep is after us and if they know where we are."

"Right." We strolled through the park, and I couldn't help but eye the people who passed us by with suspicion.

One of them could be spying on us, and we had no idea. The good thing was that I couldn't see Ethan, Rhys, and Aaron either. That meant they were well hidden, and the creep wouldn't see them and run away.

"So, is there anything interesting going on in your life?" Zack asked.

"You mean aside from all this?" I raised an eyebrow at him.

"Yeah."

"Not much. What about you?" There wasn't really time for anything else except school, and talking about school seemed boring.

He licked his lips. "I, uhm, I have a job interview. Part-time so I could still go to school."

"That's great!" A smile spread across my lips. "When?"

"Anytime I want, actually. I kind of know the guy who's hiring. He's been looking for an assistant. He fixes cars, and he said he could teach me how to work with him because he needs help."

"Awesome. But if you can just show up at any time, why haven't you done it already?" I furrowed my brow. "I mean, he basically said he'd give you the job, right? I mean, the interview thing is just a formality."

"I guess." He lowered his gaze to the ground. "But I don't know if I can do it. I've never been to a job interview or worked anything with cars. What if I mess it all up? What if I do get the job, and then I damage something? How am I going to pay for it?"

"You're overthinking it." I placed my hand on his shoulder, and his gaze met mine. "You're going to do fine, and I'm pretty sure the guy has insurance in case something breaks. And he probably won't even let you deal with something you might easily break."

"I hope so. But there's also something else." He sighed.

"What?"

"My mom. She said that if I take the job, or any job, she'd never speak to me again. She's still pretending she lives like a queen in some mansion somewhere outside town."

"I'm sorry, but your mom sounds delusional. What are you going to do? Forever pretend that you're rich? I don't get it."

"Me neither. I asked her, but she only said that we'd figure it out. But whatever she and my dad tried to do didn't work. I don't want to wait for their magical solution that probably won't happen. Except, they're my parents, and I'm going to miss them."

"That sounds like a difficult choice." My hand shifted to his back, rubbing gently. "But I think you should do what's best for you. Maybe once you have a job and your own place, your mom and dad will figure out they're wrong. You're already eighteen, right? You can do whatever you want and they can't stop you."

"I know, but it's..."

"Scary?" I offered.

He nodded. "I've never done anything like it before, and being on my own... If it wasn't for Ethan, Aaron, and Rhys, I don't know what I would've done. Ethan lets me stay at his place, and his mom and dad don't care, but I know I can't stay with him forever."

"Then go get that job. I think you've already made a decision. You just need one final push."

He watched me for a few long moments. "Yeah. I'll go. But I'm not sure when."

"How about now?"

His eyebrows shot up. "What do you mean now? Our plan is to talk and walk around the park. We can't just leave. The guy's shop is in a different direction."

"But is it far away from here?"

"Maybe about ten minutes away if we walk there."

"Then we can go." I didn't want him to get scared again and change his mind. A job was exactly what he needed. "I'm sure Ethan, Rhys, and Aaron will figure something out and follow us. We can't just walk up and down all the time as if we're waiting for someone to catch us."

"Should we ask them what they think first?" he asked.

"We can just text them where we're going."

"Okay." Zack pulled out his phone.

We slowly made our way to the shop. I kept looking around, but I didn't see anyone familiar or suspicious.

Once we got in front of the shop, Zack stopped.

"I don't know," he started to say. "Maybe it's not the right—"

"Just go." I pushed him toward the door. "You'll be fine."

He inhaled deeply and entered.

I paced up and down as I waited for him to finish. When he finally got out, his face was pale. A few seconds later, a big grin broke out on his face.

"Did you get it?" I asked, holding my breath.

"I did."

"That's amazing! Congrats!" I ran to him and threw myself into his arms.

When his arms wound around me, it was like the time had stopped. We stared into each other's eyes, our lips only inches away, and then he pressed his mouth against mine.

The kiss sent a shiver of delight down my spine, and I wrapped myself around him. He tasted so damn good, and I didn't want to stop.

Except...

I pulled away.

I shouldn't be kissing him. We'd gotten carried away, but we weren't on a real date.

"Sorry, I just..." he said.

"No, it's fine. It wasn't you. We were just... excited about your new job."

"Um, yeah." He cleared his throat.

I wondered if the rest of the boys had seen our kiss. If they were around, they probably had. And the creep...

Well, we were going to find out, weren't we?

CHAPTER 18

"How is that even possible?" I asked Ethan as we were on our way to the football field.

I was on my second date. Even though the boys had been watching Zack and me the whole time we'd been out, they hadn't seen anyone suspicious or familiar, and yet, one image of Zack and me kissing had shown up on the website.

"I don't know," Ethan said. "I swear we were watching everything and everyone carefully, but since you didn't follow our initial plan, it wasn't easy to go after you unseen. The creep must've used that."

"Well, Zack and I had a good reason to change the plan. Aren't you happy for him? I don't think he would've gone through with it if we hadn't gone there immediately."

"Yeah, of course I'm happy, but I just wish we could've seen something useful."

"Right. Then you wouldn't have had to go on a fake date with me."

His mouth opened in surprise. "No, I didn't mean it like that. I just—"

"It's fine. It's not like we're on an actual date."

Ethan looked like he was about to say something, but he must've changed his mind because he stayed quiet.

"There's going to be a lot of people here. How are we going to spot the creep?" I said when I noticed the large crowd that had gathered in front of the entrance.

"We'll have to do our best. But I think this is one of the best spots for catching that person. They'll think that no one can see them because there are so many people, so maybe they'll be less careful."

"Okay, maybe, but everyone will be able to see us. If everyone's attention is on us, how are we going to figure anything out? And someone else might take some pics too."

"We've already tried a less crowded place. And hopefully, everyone will be more interested in the game. Sure, they might look at us at first, but what do they get from staring? We're boring. Besides, this is one of the most important games of the season." Sadness filled his eyes.

"Are you okay? I know you thought you'd be playing this one with your team."

He let out a loud breath. "Yeah. I wish I could play with them, but there's nothing I can do about that now. I messed up and now they'll have to do without me. I'm sure my replacement will do a good job. Maybe even better."

"Did you turn in your essay?" I asked.

He shook his head, a small smile curving his lips.

"Why not? I thought the deadline was—"

"Oh, it's past the deadline already. I decided not to submit it."

"But you were working hard on it." We made our way to our seats.

People watched us and whispered, and I caught a glimpse of Aaron on the stands on the other side.

"Yep."

"Did you think it wasn't good enough?" I met his gaze before we sat down.

"It wasn't that. I just decided that I didn't care. Why should I do something only because my brother did it? It's pointless. If I win, it won't matter. If I don't win, it will be yet another thing I can't do as well as my brother. It's stupid. I asked myself what I really wanted, and writing an essay or entering the competition wasn't one of those things."

"Oh, okay." I could understand that.

When the team got out on the field, the crowd cheered. Ethan's face lit up instantly, and people weren't focused on us so much anymore.

Soon, Ethan was caught up in the game, and I kept eyeing the crowd. Whenever someone looked my way, I tried to see if they were taking any pics.

But a whole lot of people had phones in their hands. Some were recording the game. Some were taking selfies. It was impossible to tell if anyone was snapping pics of Ethan and me.

Ethan's loud cheering brought my attention to the field. His ex-team was winning, and I clapped my hands too.

"Yes!" Ethan yelled, and then he turned to me and wrapped his arms around me.

My whole body tingled because of his touch, and when our gazes locked, we stared deep into each other's eyes for a few long moments.

The noise seemed to fade into the background, and everyone around us just disappeared.

His mouth lowered to mine, and my lips responded to his as he kissed me. I pressed myself closer to him, but then a bright flash made us jump apart.

We both looked in the direction of the person who'd

snapped the photo, but it was just the guy who usually took photos for the school paper.

"Do you think it's him?" I asked.

"I don't think so," Ethan said. "He likes to take photos, but he already has a place to post them, and his camera is way, way better. I don't think he'd ever want to take shitty pics. He'd freak out. I once told him that he could take a photo with his phone when he said he forgot his camera, and he totally flipped out on me and ranted about how it just wasn't the same, and how people like me can't appreciate art."

"Huh. Okay. I guess it can't be him."

"His soul would hurt if he posted those photos. Trust me."

"Have you seen anyone staring at us or something?"

"Ehm, pretty much everyone."

"Then let's hope Aaron, Zack, and Rhys have seen something."

"Yeah, let's hope so." Ethan glanced at my lips, and I wondered if we were going to talk about our kiss.

Probably not.

CHAPTER 19

Once again, we'd failed.

A photo had shown up on the website, but no one had seen who had taken it. The boys had had a few suspects, but it'd all turned out to be nothing.

My next date was with Rhys. First, we went to the movies, and then for a walk.

"It was a good movie," Rhys said.

"Yeah. I loved it." I grinned. "It was totally hilarious."

"I don't think there was anyone suspicious, though. Or I just stopped paying attention."

"We should've picked a more boring movie, so we wouldn't get distracted."

"But no one could've taken a photo of us in the dark. We would've seen the flash."

"Yeah, you're right. Let's hope they'll show up now," I said.

"Yeah."

We walked for a few minutes in silence, and I realized we shouldn't just keep looking around like hawks.

"Aside from all this, what you've been up to?" I asked. "Anything interesting you'd like to share?"

"Not much. But I'm considering going to college. I just want to get away from... everything. The only problem is that my SAT scores aren't good enough, so I probably won't get a scholarship because the college I want to go to cares a lot about the scores. And if I don't get a scholarship, I'm pretty much screwed because I can't afford it. I'm already trying to save as much money as possible so I can move out, but I don't know what will happen or if my plan will work."

"You can retake the test and improve your scores," I said. "It might be too late to apply this year, but you can take a gap year and work, and then go to college."

"I don't know. Maybe it wouldn't be too late. I'd have to check. But I don't know if I can improve my scores. It just seems hopeless."

"Why would it be hopeless?"

"Because I'm hopeless at studying. I get distracted, or

I don't know how and where to start, and then I just lose interest." He averted his gaze.

It wasn't a surprise he couldn't focus on studying, considering his situation at home. "Maybe I can help you."

His eyebrows lifted up as he looked at me. "Why?"

"Why not? You need help, and I can try to find some spare time. We can meet at the library, or if you're working, we can do it there. If that's possible, of course. I could sit at the bar and bring all the notebooks and stuff."

"Yeah, that sounds good. My boss won't mind as long as I get the work done."

"Great. I'll have to look at my schedule and see if I have any exams coming up, and then I'll text you when I'm free. I hope we'll catch the creep soon because it's taking us a lot of time and energy to even figure out their identity."

"I know," Rhys said. "I just can't believe we never see them. How do they do that?"

"Maybe they're just super-stealthy. Um, is your father maybe looking into it too?" I asked.

He scoffed. "Nope. He pretends he is, of course, but he's just waiting for the case to solve itself. It's not important enough to get someone better to take a look because my dad downplayed the whole thing as just silly teenage gossip, and since we don't have a dead body or anything like that, no one else will care."

"So we're on our own? I guess the school isn't doing anything either because it's not like the website is theirs."

"Yeah. No one gives a shit."

"But what's posted on the website has serious consequences. People's lives are getting destroyed."

"Again, no one died, so not serious enough."

"Does it really have to go that far? Do we have so much bullying in schools that it kind of became normal? You don't even wanna know what the counselor said to me after you guys had that paint spilled on me."

Rhys grimaced. "I'm sorry about that. We were idiots."

"Yeah, you were."

"So what did the counselor say?"

"He basically said that he believes I did it to myself for attention."

His jaw went slack. "What?"

"I know. It's insane. So with a counselor like that, who's going to step forward and say something? No one. Because even if they did, he'd just laugh at them."

"I've spoken to him a few times. He didn't seem so bad. I can't believe he said that to you."

"Why were you sent to him? I wouldn't be surprised if he was on your side, so he was nice about it."

"I don't remember, actually. But I think it was because I told my Math teacher that her homework was stupid. It was because I was angry that I didn't manage to finish it because my dad was in a bad mood the night before. She sent me to the counselor. I expected he'd tell me off, but he joked with me and just said I shouldn't say stuff like that to her face."

"Yeah, I guess he thought the whole thing was funny. I swear if that guy has an actual diploma, it has to be fake."

"What if he's a serial killer who took on the real counselor's identity and is now having fun with us?" Rhys grinned at me. "Maybe he's the one tormenting us and trying to get inside our heads."

"Ha ha. Sounds like a TV show I watched. But I'm pretty sure our counselor wouldn't be so interested in our lives. He'd roll his eyes and say we were annoying or something."

He tensed. "Don't look," he whispered. "But someone's watching us."

"Um, okay." I stopped.

Rhys leaned closer to me while keeping his eyes on the person he'd spotted. All I could do was stare at his face. His eyes were incredibly distracting.

"False alarm," he whispered a few moments later, his gaze focusing on me.

"Uh-huh."

Our lips were so close, and I wanted more than anything to brush mine against his.

He lowered his head, and his mouth found mine. His kiss was soft and gentle at first, but then it deepened and became less hesitant.

His arms went around me, and I pulled myself closer to him.

"Why does it feel so good to kiss you?" he said quietly when we broke apart.

I bit down on my lip.

That was a good question.

It just felt right.

Rhys' phone vibrated in his pocket, and after he checked it, he scowled.

"What?" I asked.

"A photo of us is already on the website. We failed again."

"But how?"

"I don't know." He ran his hand through his hair.

The creep was incredibly slippery, or there was something we were missing.

CHAPTER 20

Aaron was still kind of on house arrest for getting kicked off the soccer team, and even though he could sneak out sometimes, we thought it was too risky for him to try to go on a date with me somewhere, especially if there were going to be photos.

So, to avoid any drama with his parents, we'd decided to have a picnic in his backyard. Okay, maybe all the food I'd brought with me for the picnic was going to be an issue with his parents anyway, but I hoped we could get away with it if they didn't look at us too closely.

Also, it shouldn't be too hard to watch the backyard, so if the creep showed up, it was more likely the boys would spot them.

"Wow, this is nice," Aaron said as he settled on the blanket next to me.

"Yeah, it is. Even if all we can see from here is the street."

Aaron glanced back at the house, and then he snatched one of the little sandwiches I'd made. He stuffed it in his mouth, and a low sound came out from the back of his throat.

"Fuck, this is amazing," he said.

"I'm glad you like it."

"My mom and dad will freak out if they see me eating this."

"Then let's hope they don't see you." I gave him a small smile. "What's up with your parents anyway? I mean, I get that they're upset you got kicked off the team, but if they're so obsessed with what you're eating—"

"It's complicated. My dad is actually searching for a new team for me. He and mom are pissed off that I ruined my chance, and now they think that every scout out there will know I was using illegal substances, and no one will ever want me. My dad got a crazy idea too."

"What idea?" I leaned closer to him.

"He wants us to move to Brazil. He wants me to change my name too so that no one can figure out who I really am. Then, he thinks I should work really hard to get noticed, and if I become famous, no one will care too much about what happened before. Actually, my dad is hoping we'll be rich enough so we can make it all go away, and no one will ever know."

"Oh. And what do you want?"

"I just want to play soccer. Now that I'm not playing, I miss it all the time, but I don't miss all the pressure. I don't want to have to impress anyone. Maybe just the people I care about." His eyes briefly met mine. "I think I'd rather go to college. Maybe I can be on their team. But nothing too professional. If I think about the famous soccer players and their lives, I don't think I want that. The fame and money sound awesome, just like playing for one of the best teams in the world, but there's just so much pressure. One bad game, one mistake, and everyone's all over you because of it. The media, the fans..."

"Yeah, that doesn't sound fun at all."

"And it's not easy to get to the top. It's a lot of work and sacrifice, and after everything that happened and seeing my secret just posted online for everyone, I'm even surer that I don't want any of it."

"Have you told your parents that?"

"I tried, like a billion times, but they refuse to listen. It's their dream, and they know I like soccer, so they don't get why I would just walk away from a potentially brilliant future that people can only dream about."

"But can't they see you were under so much pressure and that it had a negative impact on your life?"

"Not really. They think I'm an idiot and that I just don't know what's good for me, so they're going to make all the decisions for me and set me on the right path."

"But you're almost eighteen. They won't be able to make you go."

He snorted. "You don't know them. They always find a way to get what they want."

"Well, it can't be always. Their dreams aren't your dreams. You can go to college and start your own life. They won't have a say in it."

"If I can get in. I still haven't heard anything."

"I'm sure you will." I placed my hand over his.

His gaze was pinned on me, and when he leaned toward me, I didn't back away. His lips grazed mine, and a shudder of delight rushed through me.

"Hey, you! Stop!" Rhys' shout made both Aaron and me look in the direction of his voice.

A person with a black hood over their head flew down the street on a bike, and Ethan, Zack, and Rhys were trying to catch them, but they just couldn't run that fast.

Aaron and I jumped to our feet, and we hurried to them.

"Was that the creep?" I asked.

"Yeah, probably," Zack panted. "They had their phone up and aimed at you guys. But they had dark sunglasses and a hood over their head, and we don't even know what they look like."

"Do you think we could recognize the bike?" Ethan asked.

"Only if the creep goes to our school and leaves the bike outside," Rhys said. "Otherwise, probably not. We don't even know where they live or where to look."

Aaron's phone vibrated, and he pulled it out of his pocket.

"Shit," he said. "I set up an alert so I'd know whenever something gets posted on the website."

"They already posted a pic?" I asked.

"Yep," Aaron said.

"Does that mean they stopped somewhere? Or that they live in this neighborhood?"

"No clue. We should check," Zack said. "If the bike's outside, we might be able to recognize it."

"Aaron and I haven't seen it," I said.

It had all happened too fast, and we'd been too far away.

"Right. Ethan, Rhys, and I will go," Zack said. "Mel, if you want to go home, you can."

"Will you call me if you find something?" I asked.

"Yeah," he said.

I pulled out my phone and went straight to the Journal. The whole thing now seemed like a reality show or something.

The comments section was going wild. There was a new comment every few seconds. People were calling me names.

Some thought the boys were playing me because there was no way they'd be into me. Someone even suggested that I was their drug dealer, which was ridiculous.

Everyone was having fun with this, and it hadn't even occurred to them to stop and think about how this was affecting us all.

And the creep was probably having the best time of their life, thinking they're super-popular and loved, even if no one knew who they were.

It was just sick.

All of it.

And I couldn't wait for it to end.

CHAPTER 21

Finding the bike had turned out to be impossible, even though the boys were always looking, just in case it showed up somewhere.

But I had a feeling our creep was smarter than that. They'd probably gotten rid of the bike already, and once we found it, it would belong to someone completely clueless about the whole thing.

All I knew was that we shouldn't lose hope. We could just keep going on dates or try to do something else that would bring the creep straight to us.

Sam had invited me to her house so we could study together. Before I could even reach the front door of her house, she opened it wide.

"Hey." She flashed me a broad smile. "I saw you from my window."

"Hey. I brought that book you asked for," I said.

"Awesome. Come on. Let's go to my room. You have to tell me everything."

And when she said that, she meant that she wanted to hear everything about the boys. It was pretty obvious that I was hanging out with them for some reason, not to mention the pics.

Sam knew something was up, but I'd been avoiding talking about it under the excuse that someone could overhear us at school and it would only make things worse.

She had to be dying to hear all the details. If I were her, I'd want to know more too. We were best friends after all.

"So what's up with you and those four?" Sam asked the moment we entered her room.

I lowered my bag to the floor and sat down on the edge of her bed. "Um, honestly, I'm not sure."

"Oh, come on! There are photos of you kissing them, and you didn't want to tell me anything! Are you really dating all of them?"

"Maybe." I actually wasn't sure.

The boys and I had been trying to catch the creep, but we hadn't had to kiss for that. There was obviously something more between us, and I hadn't been imagining any of it. I didn't think they were playing me either.

"How the hell does that happen?" Sam's face turned serious, and I raised an eyebrow at her.

"What do you mean?" My insecurities reared their ugly heads again.

Was everyone always going to assume they were too good-looking for me? Was it such a surprise that anyone would like me?

"Well, they bullied you. They didn't trust you. They basically treated you like shit, and now you're kissing them and going on dates with them. And they're all okay with you dating all of them? Are you going to pick one or do you like them all? Are you in a poly relationship?"

"They apologized, and they're trying to show me they can be better," I said, and that was the truth. "I'm not sure about the rest. I guess I'm attracted to them, and I like them. And yes, all of them. But it's too soon to talk about a relationship."

"People are going to talk. We've never had such a relationship at our school. Usually someone gets jealous and wants their loved one just for themselves. Are you sure you want to deal with that?"

"I don't know. I guess I'm going to see what happens. I don't want to rush into anything, and you're right. I can't just trust them instantly. They need to earn my trust."

"Well, seems to me they've already earned it when you're swapping saliva with them." She pressed her lips into a tight line. "And you've been spending almost all your time with them. Don't you think they might be using you again?"

"Using me how?"

"Just think about it. Their popularity suffered a huge hit when that stuff about them was posted, but now everyone's talking about them again. And most of that talk is good for them. People think they're awesome, or are imagining themselves in a relationship with all of them. But you... Everyone hates you. They're envious of you. They want to see you fall and lose everything. They don't understand what you have that they don't."

"Then what am I supposed to do? Stay away from them so that people can be happy?"

"No, I guess not, but I think you should be careful. Don't forget who they are. And hell, it's still possible they started the whole thing, or they would've already found their mysterious person."

"They actually have some clues. They'll find the person in question."

"Ah, what clues? Did they even tell you?"

"Someone took a photo of Aaron and me. I saw that person myself."

"And? Who are they?" She tilted her head.

"I couldn't see their face or recognize them."

"So it could've been someone they hired to make you think there's really someone else. It seems to me like they're getting exactly what they want. All of it."

"Okay, you have your opinion. I have mine. Can we just focus on homework now?" I didn't want to talk about the boys anymore.

They weren't behind all this.

I was sure of it.

I'd spent enough time around them to see that they were frustrated about the whole thing, and their behavior and reactions weren't fake.

But I didn't want to tell Sam all that.

"Yeah. That's a good idea," she said. "Let me just get my notebook."

"One from your desk? Which one? I'll grab it." I got to my feet because I was closer to the desk.

"Yeah. The one with the blue cover."

"Okay." I took the notebook, and then something caught my eye.

A dinosaur sticker.

They were all over Sam's notebook.

My heart skipped a beat. I was sure it was from the

same series of stickers like the one I'd found on the floor of Rhys' room.

"Hey, where'd you get these stickers?" I asked, pointing at the notebook. "They're so cool."

"Oh, thanks! I started collecting them a while ago. They're really rare and hard to get, but my aunt lives close to the place that still sells them, and she sent me some."

"That's great." I forced my lips into a smile, but I didn't know what to think.

What were the odds that my best friend collected the same stickers as the creep?

What did this even mean? Sam couldn't be the creep. That would make no sense.

Maybe she didn't like the boys, but she wouldn't be posting stuff about other people or about me.

No, it was just impossible.

There had to be an explanation, but when I opened my mouth to ask her about it, words didn't come out.

I just didn't know what to say, or if I should even say anything before I knew more. I wanted to talk to the boys.

"Here," I said, giving her the notebook.

"Thanks! Lie down on my bed. We'll be more comfortable that way."

"Yeah, sure." I climbed onto the bed and lay on my

stomach, my notebook in front of me, and Sam settled next to me, her shoulder brushing mine.

She looked at me for a few moments and then smiled.

"Let's begin," she said.

"Yeah," I said softly, unsure how I was going to wait until we were done to talk to my boys.

CHAPTER 22

When I told the boys I needed to see them ASAP, they immediately told me they'd come, even Aaron, who said he'd sneak out.

The only problem was finding the right spot, because the creep was definitely following us, even if we couldn't see them.

And no, I didn't even want to think about the possibility that it was Sam or that she'd had something to do with the whole thing.

It was just insane.

I knew Sam.

She wasn't that person.

Finally, the boys and I agreed to meet behind the

library. I hoped no one would find us there, but it was getting late, and the school was closed.

If anyone wanted to gather and get drunk or stoned, they'd usually do it on the other side of the building. The strong smell of the trash containers was one of the main reasons why people didn't want to hang out close by.

I scrunched my nose as soon as the smell hit me, but I knew I had to keep going. Hopefully, I wouldn't end up gagging or throwing up. Some of the trash was on the ground too, so I had to sidestep it.

When I spotted the boys in the darkness, I rushed to them. Maybe all the creep wanted was to spill people's secrets, but I didn't want to be alone around here, just in case.

"Mel," Ethan said as soon as he saw me.

My boys surrounded me, and for some reason, I immediately felt safe. I supposed I didn't see them as a potential threat, even if I maybe should.

But I didn't want to think about that now. My boys weren't going to hurt me.

"What did you want to tell us so urgently"? Aaron asked. "If my mom figures out I'm not home, she's going to kill me, so this better be good."

"Remember the sticker I found on your floor?" I asked Rhys.

He nodded.

"What sticker?" Zack asked.

"I told you. It was some stupid sticker with a dinosaur," Rhys said.

"Oh yeah," Zack said. "I remember now. What about it?"

"My friend has those stickers all over her notebook."

"Samantha?" Ethan gave me an incredulous look.

"Yeah. She said those stickers are super-rare and she's collecting them. Apparently, she got them from her aunt because they don't really sell them around here." I bit down on my lip.

"What? I'm going to kill that bitch!" Zack raised his voice and was about to turn around and probably storm off, but Aaron caught his arm to stop him.

"Wait, I don't think it's her," I said. "Please hear me out."

"Mel, I know she's your friend," Rhys said. "But if she's the one who has the password, then she has to be stopped."

"Maybe she gave the stickers to someone," I said.

"Why didn't you ask her?" Zack asked.

"Don't be a dumbass," Ethan said to him. "Do you want her to know we're on to her?"

"Guys, listen to me," I said. "I'm going to try to figure

out if she gave those stickers away. Maybe someone saw them and asked her for some, and she gave it to them. We should be looking for that person because they might know something."

"What if the creep blackmailed your friend into doing it?" Aaron asked. "Does she have any secrets someone might be able to use against her?"

"As far as I know, no."

"That means nothing." Zack groaned. "If it's a big secret, she's not going to tell it to anyone, not even to her best friend."

"Maybe it *is* her," Rhys said. "What do we know? I've always thought she had a thing for Mel."

"What?" I gaped at him.

"Oh, come on," he said. "Don't you see how she always wants to be around you? And she's always looking for an excuse to touch you?"

"No! She's my friend!" I shot him a glare. "Just a friend, okay?"

"Does she think the same?" Aaron asked. "Think about it. She wanted to be with you, but we were in the way. What would be the perfect thing to do to get rid of us? Turn us against you and you against us, and then she can have you all to herself."

"That's ridiculous," I said.

"Is it?" Ethan cocked his head at me.

"You too?" I backed away from them. "Do you all think Sam's into me?"

They all nodded.

"No." I kept shaking my head. "It's not her. It can't be her. She wouldn't just do that to people. It's not just your secrets that were posted. Even if in some parallel universe your theory made sense, Sam would never hurt Ashley or anyone else. Besides, if she likes me, why let me suffer when I read all those nasty comments?"

Aaron shrugged. "So she can console you and tell you how awesome you are, and that you shouldn't listen to any of that crap because she'll be by your side and protect you?"

I just stared at him.

What they were saying wasn't true. There had to be another explanation.

But a small voice in my head was telling me that maybe they were right, and I was the one who refused to believe that Sam could do something like that.

"Okay, maybe it's not that," Rhys said. "But why don't we make sure of that?"

"How?" My voice was a little shaky.

"You could do it," Zack said. "You're with her all the time, and she won't be suspicious of you. We can follow her when you're not around, but you're the one who could check if she has access to the Journal."

"I don't know." My palms were getting sweaty, and the world was spinning lightly around me.

"You can do it," Ethan said, placing his hand on my back. "All you have to do is grab her phone and check if she's logged in. If you find nothing, then you can check her computer next. She won't be suspicious of you."

"Maybe I should just talk to her. She's my best friend," I said. "I can't just—"

"But if it's her, she'll just cover her tracks and convince you that we're trying to turn you against her," Aaron said. "We can't let that happen. And you're not really doing anything bad by opening the Journal on her phone or laptop."

"You had no trouble opening it on mine," Rhys said, his gaze piercing.

"Yeah, and it was a mistake," I said. "I don't want to do it again."

"You won't be making a mistake." Ethan rubbed gentle circles on my back, and it was so damn soothing that I leaned into him. "We need to make sure. We'll also be looking if anyone else has those dinosaur stickers. Maybe they're not as rare as Samantha thinks."

"Yeah, okay." I bobbed my head. "We'll do that."

It was the only way to make sure that Sam was innocent, even if I wasn't happy about what I had to do.

"Then we have a plan," Zack said.

Yeah, we did.

I just didn't know what I was going to do if it turned out Sam was the one. My heart would break in pieces, and I didn't even want to imagine it.

CHAPTER 23

"Are you going to the library?" I asked Sam once we were in the school hallway.

"Yeah. Why? Do you want me to get something for you?" she asked.

"Actually, I thought I could go with you."

Her eyebrows arched. "Aren't you meeting with Rhys? Or Aaron? Or Ethan? Or Zack? Or all of them?"

"No. I thought about what you said, and maybe I'll just take things very slow. They hurt me once, so I can't let them hurt me again."

"You're right about that." A smile spread across her lips.

"Hey, guys," Keith said from behind my back. "Where are you going?"

"The library," Sam said. "You coming?"

"Yeah, I don't have anything better to do," he said.

I pressed my lips together. Ugh. It would be harder to do what I was supposed to do with Keith around, or well, anyone looking over my shoulder.

"I'm looking for a specific book," Sam said. "I searched for it online, and it's supposed to be somewhere in the library, but the librarian couldn't find it. She said it was somewhere. Probably someone put it in the wrong place, and now no one knows where it is."

"Classic," Keith said. "I'll help you look for it."

"Me too," I said.

"Thanks, guys." She grinned.

Once we got to the library, Sam headed straight to the shelves, and Keith and I followed her.

"This is the book I'm looking for." Sam showed us a photo of the book on her phone.

"I'll start over there," Keith said, pointing to the shelves on our right.

"Great. Then we'll look for it over here," Sam said.

I had no idea how I was supposed to get her phone, because she pocketed it and disappeared behind one of the shelves.

As I half looked for the book, half kept an eye on Sam, I tried to come up with an excuse to get her phone, but everything seemed silly, and I wasn't about to steal it from her.

I needed it unlocked too. If Sam was the one we were looking for, even though I believed she wasn't, she would make sure no one could just see the Ember High Journal on her phone and figure out she had the password.

But as we moved forward, I noticed Sam had her phone out, and she was holding it up, as if she were trying to take a photo of someone between all the shelves. As quietly as possible, I inched closer to her.

Somehow, she felt me approach, because she turned her head in my direction and quickly lowered her phone.

I glanced above the books and saw a couple was making out in the shadows of another shelf. Had Sam been trying to take a photo of them so she could post it on the website?

Maybe.

"What are you doing? Did you find the book?" I asked.

"Nope," she said. "I was just checking how many copies of another book there are because I'm going to need that one too. Turns out there's plenty, so I don't need to worry."

"Oh, do you still have the library page open? I'd like to check something too, but the browser on my phone takes forever to open it."

"Yeah, sure." She handed me the phone.

When she focused on the shelves, I turned the phone screen away from her. I could barely stop my fingers from shaking as I closed the library page and found the link to the Ember High Journal.

I held my breath as the page loaded. My heart was pounding loudly in my chest as my gaze fell on the corner of the page.

Sam wasn't logged in as the admin. I release the breath I'd been holding.

But it wasn't over yet. I quickly closed the browser and opened her photo gallery. If she had taken a photo of the couple, it would be in there.

I hated myself for invading her privacy like this. The latest photos in her gallery were her selfies, so I quickly exited the app.

"Here," I said, offering the phone back to her.

"Did you find what you were looking for?" Her gaze was trained on me.

"Not really."

"Shame." The corners of her lips lifted up and she went back to searching for her book.

Just because there was nothing on Sam's phone didn't mean she wasn't the creep for sure. Maybe she'd logged out so she wouldn't risk the same thing that had happened to Rhys.

And maybe there weren't any photos in her gallery because I'd interrupted her and she hadn't had the chance to take them.

"Hey, Sam," I said. "Can we study together today too? I think I need some more help."

"Of course!" She turned to me, a big grin on her face. "I'd love that!"

"Sam!" Keith called, a book in his hand. "Is this the one you're looking for?"

"Yeah," she said. "I can't believe you actually found it!"

"It was in plain sight, actually," he said. "I don't know how no one saw it."

"You did." She took the book. "Thanks."

"You're welcome."

I watched Sam as she hugged the book to herself.

How well did I really know her? She was my best friend, and I knew a lot of things about her, but not everything.

Everyone had their secrets, including me.

"Mel, are you okay?" she asked, her worried eyes focused on me. "You look a little off."

She placed her hand on my arm, rubbing gently.

"I'm fine. I just have a feeling like I'm forgetting something, but I'm not sure what it is. Or if there even is something."

"Oh, that happens to me all the time. We have to remember so many things. Like, a few days ago, I planned to buy myself a new dress, but so much other stuff happened, and I just forgot." Her fingers lingered on my arm. "Will you go shopping with me? I'd like to try on the dress, and you can tell me if I look hot in it." She winked at me.

"Depends on when you're going," I said. "I promised my mom I'd do something for her first. Then we said we'd study together."

I was lying about my mom, but if the boys were right about Sam being into me, and it turned out she wasn't the creep, it would be awkward if my acceptance felt like me leading her on.

Actually, maybe I was seeing things that weren't there just because the boys had suggested it. Maybe it was nothing.

Why would everyone be into me anyway?

It was insane to even think that.

"Oh, okay." Sam's face fell, and then she turned to Keith. "What about you?"

His eyes bulged. "Me? Going shopping? Yeah, I don't think so."

"Why not?" she asked.

"Well, first, I have no clue about fashion and dresses. And second, my girlfriend wouldn't like it."

"You have a girlfriend?" Sam gaped at him. "Why don't I know that?"

He shrugged. "It just never came up, I guess."

"Tell me more about her." Sam wound her arm around Keith's shoulders.

Why was she so interested in Keith's girlfriend all of a sudden? Was it because she was looking for some juicy info that she could post?

I watched them as they headed to check out Sam's book, and I realized one thing. I so didn't want the boys to be right about Sam.

CHAPTER 24

"Where are you now?" Ethan asked from the other end of the line.

"I'm on my way to Sam's house. We agreed that I'd study with her again." I clutched my phone in my hand.

"What happened?" I heard Aaron's voice in the background.

"I had her phone, but I didn't find anything."

"Maybe she won't even be logged in," Ethan said. "You'll have to look for something else. If she's the one, she has to have the photos and other information stored somewhere. If the anonymous submissions aren't saved, they get deleted when they reach a certain limit. I don't think she'd just let that happen if she always wanted to have some material for the website."

"Okay, can you stop talking about it like she's definitely the one?" I said. "It makes me uncomfortable."

"Yeah, if that's what you want. I didn't mean that she was a hundred percent guilty. We're just considering her as a suspect," he said.

"Um, yeah, and when you were doing it to me, it didn't really go well. If only you'd given me the benefit of the doubt first."

"Sorry. We weren't really thinking about it like that."

"Yeah, you were only thinking about yourselves, but whatever." I didn't want to get into that right now.

Glancing around, I made sure no one was close enough to me to be able to overhear me.

"Again, sorry for that."

"What were you saying about the website?" I asked. "If I'm going to be able to use her computer, then maybe I can look for whatever you think that should be there if she's the one. Then I can prove it's not her."

"There would be some logs on her computer, but I don't think you can find them easily if you don't know what you're looking for," Rhys said.

"Great. You could've told me that earlier and shown me."

"It doesn't matter. The files are what matters. She has to have them stored somewhere. Do you know how to look for hidden folders and files?" he asked. "Also, if she saves them directly without changing the name, the title will include the date and time when the file was received, so you should look for the files like that."

"Yeah, I think I can manage that, but it'll be hard to do it. I can't exactly snoop through her computer for hours."

"Can you copy her drive?" Aaron asked.

"I'm not doing that!"

"But you're okay with searching through her files?"

"Yeah. It's wrong too, but I want to prove that she has nothing to do with the website, and I won't be keeping a copy of her files or reading anything I shouldn't. I'll just look for what you said I should look. If I make a copy, then all her personal files will be there, and if whoever has that drive can access them... Well, you know. So no, I'm not doing that. I'll search, but that's all."

"Okay," Rhys said. "If you need any help, just text me. I'll guide you through it or help you figure out if it might be the right file."

"Yeah."

"Just promise you'll be careful," Ethan said. "If she catches you, and she's the person we're looking for, you might be in trouble."

"We should be close by," Zack said. "We can't let her do this alone."

"Yeah, you're right," Aaron said.

"I can hear you," I pointed out.

"As Zack said, we're going to be close in case you need us," Aaron said. "Only a call away."

"I'll be perfectly safe. If Sam is in love with me or something, like you think she is, then she won't hurt me." I had no idea why they were worried about me.

It wasn't like I was going to visit some dangerous criminal.

It was my best friend.

"All right," Aaron said. "But we'll be there anyway, even if it's just so we can hear everything you found out as soon as possible."

"Fine. I have to go. I'm almost there." I ended the call and slipped my phone back into my pocket.

I'd prove Sam was innocent.

When I was in the middle of her driveway, she opened the door. Was she always waiting for me to show up?

"My mom baked some cookies before she left," she said. "You're going to love them."

"Can't wait." I flashed her a smile.

Once we were in her room and had our books out, I clamped my hand over my mouth.

"Oh, shit," I said.

"What's wrong?" Sam was instantly alert.

"I was supposed to send an email to my cousin. She

wanted me to help her with something. She's going to kill me." I groaned.

"Um, if you have what you need here, you can just send it now. I can wait."

"I would, but I need to download some pics, and I'm pretty sure my phone can't handle any of that. It would take hours."

"That's not a problem either. You can use my laptop." She got to her feet and grabbed her laptop.

"Are you sure? I don't want to—"

"Oh please, are we friends or not? Here." She set the laptop in front of me. "I'll go get us those cookies."

"Sounds great! Thanks." I gave her a big smile.

When she was gone, I quickly brought up the web browser. The first thing I opened was the Ember High Journal.

She wasn't logged in.

Then I started searching for the recent files, quickly going through their names.

Nothing suspicious there.

Relief flooded me.

It wasn't her. There was nothing to be found.

I quickly deleted my search history so she wouldn't know what I'd been doing, just a moment before she returned.

"You're a lifesaver," I said. "All done."

"Great!" She set a plate of delicious-looking cookies in front of me. "I'm going to get myself a glass of milk too. Do you want some?"

"No, thanks."

Once she was gone, I pulled out my phone and texted the boys to let them know that I'd found nothing, as expected.

But they texted me back telling me that there might be another secret computer or a phone in the house.

I inwardly groaned.

They were being ridiculous.

But I could entertain their fantasy for a bit. If Sam had a secret computer, where would she keep it?

Probably not anywhere her parents might see it, because they'd probably ask her why she had it. She couldn't be hiding it anywhere there might look.

The attic!

I remembered the attic. Sam had told me once no one ever went there and that her parents had completely forgotten about it, even though she wanted to use it as an extra room or even a small library.

Okay, I could check the damn place, even if I got some dust and cobwebs all over me for nothing.

"I'm going to the bathroom," I yelled to Sam so she wouldn't wonder where I'd gone.

"Okay!" she yelled back.

I padded down the hallway and found my way to the attic.

As quietly as possible, I climbed the creaky stairs and opened the door. A musty smell hit me, but the room was much cleaner than I'd thought it would be, and there were a whole lot of things lying around.

I sighed as the door closed behind me.

How the hell was I supposed to be quick enough to search through all this?

CHAPTER 25

I was just taking a peek into one of the open boxes when I heard footsteps outside, and they were coming closer.

Had Sam figured out where I'd gone?

Maybe. But why wasn't she calling for me then?

I backed away from the door, looking for a place to hide. If she didn't see me, she'd go away, and then I wouldn't have to explain that the boys had convinced me that I should investigate her because they believed she was the creep and also in love with me.

Yep, just thinking about it sounded ridiculous. I didn't think she'd forgive me if she found out.

I was a terrible friend. If she suspected me like this and didn't tell me anything, I would be furious. Going through her computer had already been bad enough. Now I was just making things worse.

I ducked behind an old armchair, barely able to fit in between the boxes. Holding my breath, I listened as the footsteps grew louder and louder.

The door opened.

If Sam got inside and saw me, maybe I could pretend I was playing hide and seek. She'd be weirded out, but maybe she'd go along with it.

A few moments later, the door closed. I waited until the footsteps could no longer be heard.

Okay, I'd have to come up with some explanation for Sam. Maybe I could say mom had called and that I'd had to step outside for a bit so I could talk to her.

As I was getting to my feet, I focused on the box that was right next to me. It looked different from the others.

Newer, somehow, and without any dust.

It was closed, but I managed to open it.

My eyes widened.

Photos and notes.

And a phone.

My pulse sped up as I picked up the phone. It was off, and when I turned it on, it required a password and a fingerprint scan.

Shit. I wasn't going to be able to unlock it.

But as I picked up the photos and looked through

them, my hands started shaking. There were printed out images of everything that had been posted on the website, and there were some that I hadn't seen.

More images of me and the boys.

More images of me.

Of other people too.

I picked up the notes. They were handwritten.

What the hell?

I read through a few of them and recognized them. All of that stuff had been posted on the website, probably word for word.

Why did Sam have all this in here?

Maybe because we'd all been looking for a file on her computer while she actually had everything stored in here. She couldn't have just taken that stuff off the website, printed it out, and kept it for some weird reason because a lot of it hadn't actually been posted.

There was only one explanation for this.

Except...

I stared at the notes.

The handwriting wasn't hers.

It wasn't.

Unless she'd somehow changed her style. I took one of the notes and stuffed it in my pocket, and returned the rest of the stuff into the box. As carefully as possible, I put the things back as they'd been.

I hurried to the door, half expecting Sam to be waiting for me in the hallway, but no one was there, so I almost ran back to Sam's room, trying to come up with an explanation.

I should probably tell her what I'd found and ask what the hell was going on. She was my friend, dammit. We could talk about this.

She wasn't going to do anything to me, and maybe there was something else going on. Someone could be blackmailing her.

I refused to believe she would just run that damn website without caring about the effect it had on everyone, including me.

"Mel, someone's at the door," Sam yelled. "I'll be right back."

"Okay," I shouted back.

A few moments later, she and Keith appeared at the door.

Shit. Now I couldn't ask her anything, could I?

"Hey," Keith said. "Sam told me you two could use another study partner."

"Um, I guess." I glanced at Sam, who was only smiling at me.

Why hadn't she told me?

Or had she wanted someone else in the house so I

wouldn't have the time to accidentally stumble on some damning evidence against her?

Keith got his stuff out of his bag and put it on the bed. "Do you have something to eat? I'm starving. Didn't get a chance to grab myself anything."

"I'll make you a sandwich," Sam said.

"I can do it myself. Just show me where the food is. I don't want to trouble you," he said.

"It's not a problem, but you can come help me."

"Okay." He followed her out.

When they were gone, I grabbed the note from my pocket and put it next to one of Sam's notebooks.

Definitely not her handwriting.

Not at all.

That was just weird.

My gaze fell on Keith's notebook and his name written on it.

My shoulders stiffened.

Shit!

I reached for his notebook and opened it, and then compared it with the note.

It was his! It was his handwriting!

But how had his stuff gotten into Sam's attic? Unless they were both in on it.

No! I slid my hand into my pocket to get my phone

so I could text the boys. I had no idea what was going on, but I wasn't about to stay here with them.

Not until things got cleared up.

Before my fingers could wrap around my phone, I heard the door slam closed.

I turned my head.

Keith stood in the doorway, a serious look on his face.

And then his lips pulled up into a small smile, his gaze briefly falling on the note and his open notebook on the bed.

"Looks like you know too much," he said, and locked the door.

Then he whipped out a gun and pointed it straight at me.